ABOMINABLE

DREAMWORKS

PEARL

MOVIE NOVELIZATION

DREAMWORKS

ABOMINABLE

PEARL

MOVIE NOVELIZATION

Adapted by Tracey West

SUMMIT FREE PUBLIC LIBRARY

Simon Spotlight
New York   London   Toronto   Sydney   New Delhi

This book is a work of fiction. Any references to historical events, real people, or real places are used fictitiously. Other names, characters, places, and events are products of the author's imagination, and any resemblance to actual events or places or persons, living or dead, is entirely coincidental.

SIMON SPOTLIGHT
An imprint of Simon & Schuster Children's Publishing Division
1230 Avenue of the Americas, New York, New York 10020
This Simon Spotlight edition August 2019
© 2019 Universal Studios and Shanghai Pearl Studio Film and Television Technology Co. All Rights Reserved.
All rights reserved, including the right of reproduction in whole or in part in any form. SIMON SPOTLIGHT and colophon are registered trademarks of Simon & Schuster, Inc. For information about special discounts for bulk purchases, please contact Simon & Schuster Special Sales at 1-866-506-1949 or business@simonandschuster.com.
Book designed by Nick Sciacca
The text of this book was set in ITC Stone Informal STD.
Manufactured in the United States of America 0719 OFF
10 9 8 7 6 5 4 3 2 1
ISBN 978-1-5344-4565-9 (pbk)
ISBN 978-1-5344-4567-3 (eBook)

DreamWorks

ABOMINABLE

PEARL

MOVIE NOVELIZATION

Chapter One
The Escape

The light from Dr. Zara's lab was a bright spot in the dark research facility deep in the basement of Burnish Industries. She sat at her desk with Duchess, her pet jerboa, perched on her shoulder. The white rodent's tiny ears twitched at the sound of the squawks and twitters coming from the lab animals in the neighboring rooms.

Dr. Zara tapped a pen on her desk as she spoke on the phone in a crisp British accent.

"Yes, Mr. Burnish, the venue is completely sold out," she assured him. "This is the most important discovery of the century and *everyone* wants to see it."

She spun around in her chair, putting her back to the door.

"Yes, the press will be there," she continued. "This is your big day, Mr. Burnish. You won't be disappointed. I promise."

Duchess wrinkled her nose and turned to face the door. Her black eyes widened and she squeaked in alarm.

Dr. Zara felt a prickle on the back of her neck. She slowly turned to see the hulking, furry form of a giant white beast in the doorway, standing on all fours. How had he gotten out of his cage?

She leaped to her feet. "Easy, boy . . ." She held up both hands and slowly edged toward the alarm. The beast was still, staring at her with his icy blue eyes. Was that anger she saw in them, or fear?

She hit the alarm.

Wee-oo! Wee-oo! Wee-ooo!

Techs in white coats poured into the lab, rushing toward the beast from all sides. Each one held a long metal stick with a forked end—an electric shock prod.

"Who left the enclosure open?" Dr. Zara yelled.

"Stay back!" the security captain warned.

The beast moved quickly, pushed past the guards, and raced into the hallway. Red lights flashed in the corridor. Doors slammed behind him as he bolted toward the exit door. With one last burst of energy, he broke through the door and ran into the yard.

Cold rain hit his fur and he stopped, gaining his bearings. Wire fences hemmed him in, and bright searchlights swept back and forth, trying to find him.

He ran around the yard, searching for a way out. The armed security guards surrounded him again, and this time he was trapped. He backed up against the fence and got a shock. He saw the lightning-bolt-shaped sign on it. The beast knew what that meant. If he tried to climb the fence, he'd be zapped.

Dr. Zara stepped through the guards and slowly approached him. Growling, the beast paced back and forth on his hands and feet, keeping his eyes on her.

"All right, move in slowly," Dr. Zara told the guards. "No sudden movements."

Frightened, little Duchess hid under the doctor's ponytail.

The beast's growl suddenly changed into a low, vibrating hum. His fur began to pulse with a bluish light. Dr. Zara's eyes widened with fear.

"What's happening?"

Crash! A bolt of lightning stuck one of the search-lights overhead, raining glass down on the yard. Instinctively, Dr. Zara covered her head with her hands and ran for cover under the safety of the over-hang near the door. The guards did the same.

Dr. Zara turned back toward the beast . . . but he was gone. A massive hole gaped in the mangled metal fence, showing the bright lights of a bustling Chinese city in the distance.

"Who's telling Mr. Burnish?" the security captain asked.

Dr. Zara glared at him. Mr. Burnish was not going to be happy.

She had to find the beast, and fast. Failure was not an option.

Chapter Two
Yi's Busy Day

The cold rain continued to fall as the beast ran through the city, lost and confused. Neon lights and traffic lights flashed, and impatient drivers honked their horns as they drove down the crowded streets. Thanks to the dark and the rain, none of them noticed the furry white beast racing through the metropolis.

A truck whizzed by, grazing him, and the wounded beast darted into a dark alley to escape. He gazed up at the twelve-story apartment building next to him and began to climb it. Exhausted, he collapsed into the shadows of the roof.

He faced a huge Jumbotron a few streets away that projected an image of a beautiful snow-capped mountain. The tallest mountain in the world, Mount Everest. He gazed at it as long as he could, until he drifted off into a deep sleep.

The rain stopped overnight, and the morning dawned with a bright sun in the blue summer sky. Inside the apartment building, a few floors below the sleeping beast, sixteen-year-old Yi was ready to start her day. She put on her sunglasses and opened her bedroom door. She breezed past her mom, who was packing her briefcase for work, and NaiNai making tea in the kitchen.

"Bye everybody! Have a great day!" she called over her shoulder.

"Hey! What are you? A famous person now?" NaiNai asked. Yi reluctantly took off her sunglasses.

"Where are you going?" her mom asked.

Yi paused at the door. "I've got stuff to do."

Her grandmother frowned. "Stuff? What is this stuff?" NaiNai asked. "It's a summer holiday. Either be busy or be on holiday, that is what I say."

Her mom interrupted. "Be careful out there."

"Of course!" Yi reached for the doorknob.

"Be back before dinner," NaiNai said.

"I'll try," Yi promised.

"Warm enough?" Mom asked.

"Toasty!" Yi confirmed.

"No boys!" NaiNai added.

"What?" *Why is she saying that all of a sudden?* Yi wondered. "No . . . no boys."

"Do you need any money?" Mom asked.

Yi put her sunglasses back on and confidently peered at her mom and grandmother over the top of them. "Mom, NaiNai, I've got it covered. Goodbye!"

Before they could say another word, Yi slipped out the door, but her backpack remained behind, hung up on the door handle. She tugged frantically until she managed to pull it free and then, with glasses crooked on her face, she gave a sheepish "Bye!" and escaped.

NaiNai shook her head. "What do you think she does all day?" she wondered aloud.

Yi heard her grandmother ask the question. It was one Yi knew she wasn't ready to answer. Mom and NaiNai wouldn't understand.

"All right," she told herself. "Time to get busy!"

Twenty minutes later, she walked down the street,

being pulled by a dozen dachshunds, each attached to a leash. She wove through the crowd of pedestrians and bicyclists, at the mercy of the dogs. But it was worth it when, one hour later, she delivered them back to Mrs. Zhao and received a handful of cash for her trouble.

Next stop was babysitting a four-year-old terror who thought Yi was his sworn enemy and constantly pelted her with food. After that, she washed a neighbor's car, then headed to Mrs. Chen's fish shop and spent an hour tossing cans full of slimy, smelly fish guts into the dumpster. As usual, it seemed like more guts ended up on her than in the dumpster.

By the end of the day, she was covered in fish slime and still had some of the child's breakfast porridge in her hair. But her handful of cash had grown into a nice wad, and she counted it as she headed back home.

The sound of familiar voices stopped her. Yi looked up and her smile faded. Why did she have to run into Jin now, looking like this? And of course he was with the popular kids from his class, the ones who looked like fashion models. But then again, so did Jin, with his perfectly styled hair, brand-new jeans, striped shirt, and favorite accessory: his cell phone.

"So Jin, are you going to Shuo's this weekend?" one of the girls asked him.

"Nah, I'm headed to Beijing to check out my school," he said. "I'm pre-med."

"Med school?" asked another girl.

"Wow!" said the first girl.

Jin nodded. "I know, right?"

One of the girls in the group sniffed the air. "Ugh, what is that smell?"

That smell is me, Yi realized, and she owned it. She straightened up and slipped on her sunglasses, locking eyes with Jin as he passed.

Then she heard one of the girls whisper to Jin. "She looks like she slept in a dumpster."

Everyone laughed. Even Jin. Yi scowled and kept on her way. Later that afternoon when she arrived home, she found Peng dribbling a basketball on the sidewalk.

"He breaks left. He breaks right. He's going in for the dunk!" the nine-year-old narrated, as he dribbled toward the basketball hoop in the alley. He tossed the ball at the basket, but it bounced off the pole and careened away from him. He scrambled after it and then smiled when he noticed Yi standing there.

"Hey, Yi, come shoot hoops with me!" he urged. "Come on!"

"Sorry, Peng, I don't have time," Yi replied. "Why don't you ask the other kids?"

She opened the door and started up the stairs. Peng followed her.

"The other kids are too little," Peng replied. Then he lowered his voice. "And some of them are freakishly good. Come on, Yi. You never play with me anymore."

Yi sighed. "Peng, I've been busy all day."

A little while later, Jin came out of his apartment, talking on his phone. *He must have passed me without me even noticing him*, Yi thought. Yi nodded toward him. "Your cousin will play with you."

Peng rolled his eyes. "As usual, he's got a date," he said. He puckered his lips and made silly smooching noises.

Yi laughed and kept moving up the stairs. Peng continued to follow and tugged on her shirt. "Wait, wait, Yi, here we go," he said, pointing at Jin, who was passing a window in the hallway. "Three, two, one . . . stop and check!"

On cue, Jin stopped to check out his hair in the reflection. Yi and Peng burst out laughing.

"Hey Yi, you know I can smell you from all the way over here, right?" Jin asked, not taking his eyes off his reflection.

"Like you can talk!" Yi called down the stairwell. "I'm sorry, is there any aftershave left, or did you use the whole bottle?"

Jin stepped away from the window. "Why, you hoping to borrow some? Not sure it'll help."

Yi scoffed. "Very funny."

Peng bounced the basketball on the landing. "You guys want to work out some of this tension on the court?"

"Forget it, Peng. We wouldn't want to mess up Jin's hair," Yi said scornfully.

Jin lifted a foot. "And the new kicks. No basketball for these babies." He snapped a photo of his sneakers, then turned to Peng. "Another time, okay, cuz?"

Peng sighed. "That's what you always say."

Jin headed downstairs, his eyes on his phone. "Forty-eight likes already! Sweet!"

Yi rolled her eyes. When they were kids, Yi and Jin had been best friends. They'd played together every day. But things were different now, and not just with Jin. Everything was different.

Dejected, Peng went back downstairs. Before entering, Yi paused at her apartment door, listening to Mom and NaiNai talk about her in the kitchen.

"She's never home anymore!" NaiNai complained.

"Ma . . . ," Yi's mom began.

"What? Are we just going to give up on her?" NaiNai asked.

"I'd never give up on Yi," her mom said firmly. "Look, we both know what she's been going through. She misses her dad. . . . We all do."

Yi slowly and quietly opened the door. She tiptoed through the living room, hoping to get past her mom and grandmother without being noticed.

"If we're patient and don't push her, then maybe—" Her mom stopped as Yi's foot hit a creaky floorboard.

"Yi, is that you?" NaiNai asked. "We've been waiting for you to eat."

Yi stopped. "Oh, I ate on my way back. So I'm good," she lied.

Her mom approached her. "Hey, Yi. Why don't we all sit down together tonight as a family?"

"Family?" Yi asked. Had her mom really just used that word?

"You need to eat," NaiNai called from the table. "You don't want to be so short like your mother."

"I'm okay," Yi assured her. "Thank you, NaiNai."

"Yi, wait," her mom said. "What would you say to playing a little violin for us after supper? Remember when you used to . . ."

Yi's stomach sank. "I . . . I can't."

"Can't? Why?" Mom asked.

"Because, I . . ." A thousand excuses ran through her mind. What did it matter? What did *anything* matter anymore? "I sold it. I'm sorry."

As her mom turned to go, the look of shocked disappointment on her face was enough to break Yi's heart. She stepped into her bedroom and shut the door behind her with a groan.

"Ugh!"

She didn't talk to her mom and NaiNai for the rest of the night. She showered off the fish guts and porridge, changed her clothes, then climbed into bed.

Her mom came in to check on Yi, as she did every night like clockwork. Yi kept her eyes closed as she felt her mom's hand brush her cheek. Then her mom sighed softly and quietly left the room.

When she heard the door close, Yi's eyes snapped open. She jumped out of bed and went to the window, opening it. The bright city lights obscured the stars, but she could still make out a slender crescent moon in the sky.

She climbed out of the window, onto the bamboo stairs, then made her way up to the roof.

Chapter Three
The Creature

Yi hopped off the scaffolding onto the roof. Under the bright lights of the city, she made her way to a ramshackle-looking fort built from scraps of sheet metal, wood boards, and a canvas tarp.

She pulled aside the tarp and entered. The inside looked a lot more comfortable than the outside, and that was on purpose. It was Yi's haven, her own special, secret place. Pillows were propped in the corners. A bulletin board on the wall held a large map of China adorned with colorful postcards from places all across the country. A flowerpot held a half-dead pink orchid with drooping leaves.

Yi took a stack of cash from her backpack and looked up at the map with a sigh. "I will take this trip . . . someday." She picked up the flowerpot to reveal a small hole in the floor that held the cash from her previous jobs. She added the new bills to the pile and placed the pot back down.

Then Yi pulled a battered violin case from behind the pillows and took it outside. When she opened the case, a photo of her and her dad was prominently placed inside the lid. In the photo, Yi was smiling, and her dad was holding the violin—the same one in the case. It was a beautiful memory, and a painful one too, because she knew there could never again be another moment like that.

Yi picked up the violin and stepped up onto an old fruit crate. She propped the violin under her chin, closed her eyes, and began to play. A sweet, powerful melody spilled out across the roof and over the city skyline. When Yi played, she could *feel* her dad inside the music. For a few minutes, it was like he was alive again.

Suddenly, the roar of a helicopter engine interrupted the song, and Yi opened her eyes to see a helicopter overhead, scanning the rooftops with bright searchlights. Startled, she toppled off the crate, and the violin dropped from her hands and skidded across the roof.

As the helicopter moved away, Yi reached down to grab her violin from behind the heating duct where it had landed. She stopped.

Something furry was sticking out from behind the heating duct, right next to the violin. A rat? She squinted. No, it looked like . . . a furry white hand? A mitten maybe? Or a person in a costume? But what would anybody be doing on the roof? Nobody else ever came up here.

Heart pounding, Yi considered her options. She should run. But she couldn't leave the violin behind. Cautiously, quietly, she tiptoed toward the instrument. Her fingers touched it. . . .

Twang! She accidentally plucked one of the strings. Two bright blue eyes flashed open behind the duct.

Yi jumped back. A huge beast, twice as tall as she was, jumped out at her. Its body was covered with matted white fur. It opened its mouth to roar, revealing a mouth full of sharp teeth.

Yi backed up toward the edge of the roof, too

terrified to scream. What *was* this thing? A white gorilla? A demon? Whatever it was, it didn't seem friendly!

She expected the creature to lunge at her, but it did something different. It slowly stepped toward her and made a noise again—but Yi realized it wasn't a roar, but a moan. Was something wrong? Then she noticed a large red gash on its forearm.

Whirrrrrrrrr. The helicopter was circling back toward them. The creature looked up, panicked, and limped back toward the safety of the shadows.

Yi quickly figured out the situation. The beast wasn't dangerous—if it were, it would have hurt her by now, but instead, it was hurt, and the people in the helicopter were looking for it. Were they going to hurt it again?

Without hesitation, Yi sprang into action. She dragged a sheet of scrap metal over to the beast and covered it before the helicopter passed. Then she jumped into a wooden crate and hid, watching.

The helicopter hovered for a few moments, then moved on. When it was out of sight, she emerged from the crate and peeked behind the metal sheet. The beast was asleep.

Slowly, carefully, she backed away from it. Her heart was racing, but she didn't leave the roof. This beast had a story—and she wanted to figure it out. She sat down with her back to the crate, eyes locked on the beast. This was both the scariest and most thrilling moment of her life.

Yi woke at sunrise. It took her a few seconds to realize she had fallen asleep on the roof. She rubbed her eyes and wondered if last night had all been a dream.

But just then, she heard the beast snoring behind the sheet metal. She crept up to the hiding place and peeked in. It was still asleep, and the wound on its arm didn't look any better.

Filled with compassion, Yi darted over to her fort, put the violin away, and grabbed some cash from under the flowerpot. She ran through her bedroom into the kitchen, and waved to her grandmother.

"Bye, NaiNai!"

Outside, she made a beeline for the pharmacy and bought some ointment and bandages. She hurried, because she wanted to get back before the creature woke up.

On the way home, a commotion on the street made her pause. Behind yellow caution tape, a bunch of people in lab coats were inspecting a van. Yi ducked into the nearest alley and watched. A dent in the hood of the van looked like a giant pawprint.

Just like the paws of the beast on the roof.

A red-haired woman, who appeared to be in charge of the lab coats, was questioning the van driver. Yi noticed that the woman had a jerboa on her shoulder.

Weird! Yi thought.

"Bam! It came out of nowhere. Then it was gone," the driver was saying.

"Did you see where it went?" the woman asked.

"Lady, I just told you," the driver replied. "It was gone. What was that thing, anyway?"

The woman didn't answer his question directly. "Let me take care of the damage to your truck," she said, and she waved one of the security guys over. He opened a briefcase filled with money!

"It's a bribe," the security guard said.

They're looking for the beast on my roof! Yi realized, and she ran back into the apartment as fast as she could. Passing the kitchen, she saw a fresh batch of pork buns cooling on the counter. She stuffed a few into her backpack and then turned—to see NaiNai glaring at her, her arms folded.

"So you're hungry now?" NaiNai asked.

"Um, yeah. Starving," Yi said, which wasn't a lie. She hadn't eaten since lunch yesterday, so she planned to share the buns with the beast.

"Let them cool," NaiNai said. "You'll burn your mouth."

She picked up another tray of pork buns and placed them on the cooling rack. "I keep telling your mother you need to slow down. Spend more time here at home with your family."

Yi reached for another bun, and NaiNai slapped her hand away. "Mrs. Lui called me today, says you're fixing her computer. And Mrs. Yuan in 4B said you're going to trim her poodle's toenails. I like that you're ambitious. No one wants a lazy grand-daughter. But . . . busy, busy, busy! What do you need to do all that for?"

Yi backed away, toward her bedroom. "I guess I just like being busy!" she said. "Can we talk about this later, NaiNai? You don't have to worry."

Yi ducked into her bedroom and shut the door,

not waiting for an answer. Then she climbed back up onto the rooftop, relieved to hear the beast still snoring.

She approached the hiding place. "Hey boy . . . or girl. Are you hungry?"

She dumped a pile of pork buns by the opening of the metal lean-to and waited. The snoring stopped and Yi heard the sound of sniffing. A giant, furry paw reached out and grabbed the entire pile.

Yi heard chewing sounds, and then a very loud burp.

"Yeah, you're definitely a boy," she said, wrinkling her nose as the burp stench wafted past her.

Next, Yi took the bandages and ointment from her backpack. Taking a deep breath, she slowly stepped behind the metal sheet.

The creature stared at her, suspicion in his blue eyes. She held up the bandages and moved toward his arm. He pulled it away with a snarl. Undaunted, Yi reached out again.

This time, the creature didn't move. He kept his eyes locked on Yi as she put ointment on the wound, then wrapped a bandage around it. When she finished, he yawned. His eyes drooped, and he fell into a deep sleep again.

Yi studied his face. This was no gorilla. She held her hand up against his huge, furry paw. Her hand looked tiny compared to it.

"Whoa," she said. "I don't know where you came from, but you sure don't belong here."

She glanced over her shoulder. "You stay in here, okay? There are people looking for you."

She stepped outside the lean-to and examined it. It was a decent hiding spot, but it would have to be better. She began to fortify it with items from her fort: some old posters, pillows, two broken chairs, the canvas tarp, and some holiday lights that she plugged into an outlet in the wall. Finally, she placed the drooping orchid by the entrance. One of the last petals fell off, and she sighed.

"Sorry, it's all I've got," she said.

Inside the shelter, the beast was awake. He tried to stand up using his wounded arm and whimpered. She rushed to him.

"No, no, no, it's okay," she said. "Please don't cry . . . wait!"

She retrieved her violin. "My dad used to play

for me. It always made me feel better."

Yi began to play. To her amazement, after a few bars the creature began to hum along to the melody.

It's a duet! She smiled, and she closed her eyes, lost in the music. She didn't see the blue light that glowed from the creature as he hummed. When the song ended, she looked at the beast. He had stopped crying.

She smiled. "All better, right?"

He had already fallen back to sleep. She stepped out of the shelter, past the orchid, and stopped. The upright green stem supported a beautiful new pink bloom. She looked back at the creature. Was there some connection?

"Nah," she told herself. She closed the canvas to the shelter entrance behind her.

To her surprise, the creature pulled it back. He was staring out into the city. Yi followed his gaze . . . to the giant image of Mount Everest on the Jumbotron. "Wait, do you know that place?" Yi asked, excitement rising. "Is that . . . is that your home?"

She put her fingertips together to make a triangle shape with her hands. "You know. Home."

The creature made the same shape with his hands, then made a cooing sound.

Yi's eyes widened. She pulled out her phone and began to type "Creature from Mount Everest . . ."

She read the first entry out loud. "Considered to be no more than fairy tale and myth, enthusiasts still hold out hope that these creatures actually do exist."

She gasped. "There's a yeti on my roof!"

Chapter Four
The Chase

"Where's my yeti?" Mr. Burnish thundered.

The angry billionaire sat behind his desk in his penthouse office, shouting into his speakerphone. "Captain, I am holding you personally responsible for that abominable creature's escape! Now you will get every car we have out of there, or I will send you back to your job at the shopping mall."

His loud voice blared from the cell phone of the security captain, who was riding shotgun in a company SUV, searching the city streets for the yeti. Dr. Zara sat in the back, and Duchess anxiously paced back and forth along the top of the seats.

"Yes sir, understood," the captain replied. Then he spoke into his headset. "Attention all units. We need every car out on the street!"

A yeti. Yi's mind was spinning. She had spent the day anxiously watching over him—it seemed all he wanted to do was sleep. Then she heard his stomach rumble, and Yi knew he needed more pork buns—lots of them. If she took more from NaiNai, her grandmother would get suspicious.

"I'll be right back," she promised, and she climbed back down into the apartment, then headed out to buy some pork buns with her own money. There was a long wait at the shops, and she tapped her foot impatiently while she waited in line. It didn't feel right, leaving the yeti alone for so long. Sure, he was a big, hairy beast, but there was something really vulnerable about him. He needed protecting.

She finally got the buns and headed home. Peng spotted her coming back and followed her into the apartment building.

"I was dribbling and the guy was like, 'Oh no!'

and I was like, 'Oh yeah!'" he bragged. "Want to play a game?"

"I can't," Yi said. "NaiNai will, though."

Yi headed straight for her room and hurried back up to the roof. When she arrived, she found the yeti outside the shelter, cooling in front of a window-unit air conditioner—the air conditioner from her family's living room!

"Hey, what are you doing out here?" she asked. "Someone's going to see you!"

Yi put her arms around the air conditioner, and so did the yeti. They played tug-of-war with the machine. "Do you hear me? Let go!"

Suddenly Yi heard keys in the access door to the roof. There was no time to hide the yeti. The door opened—and Jin and Peng stepped out!

"Ahhhhhhhhhh!" Peng screamed.

Jin picked up a broken chair.

"Uh, guys, what are you doing up here?" Yi asked.

Jin yelled at the yeti. "Get away from her!"

"No, no, no!" Yi cried. "Wait!"

Jin pulled out his phone. "I'm calling the police."

"Wait Jin, *no*!" Yi pleaded. "Hang up!"

But Jin had already dialed. "Hello, hello? Yes,

there's a wild beast on our roof. Send help!"

Jin's voice crackled on every police scanner around the city. Everyone tuned in to a police scanner heard it—including Dr. Zara.

"Jin, what have you done?" Yi shouted. "He's not dangerous. Look at him. He's a yeti."

Peng's face lit up. "Cool!"

Jin cried out. "What?! No! Yetis don't exist!"

At that moment, a helicopter emblazoned with a Burnish Industries logo rose up over the roof.

"Oh no. They're back!" Yi cried. She turned to the yeti. "You have to go."

Frightened, he just stared at her.

"Go, run. Now! Go!" Yi pleaded.

The wind caused by the whirring chopper blades sent the contents of the shelter scattering across the roof . . . pillows, maps, and postcards.

"No, no, no, no!" Yi scrambled to catch the postcards before they blew away, grab her violin, and stow everything into her backpack.

Then she felt a pair of furry arms around her waist as the yeti hoisted her onto his back. Before she could react, he leaped onto the next rooftop, taking her with him. Yi heard her friends as she was carried off.

"He stole Yi!" Peng cried.

"More like kidnapped!" Jin said. "Come on, Peng!"

Yi clung to the yeti's back, too terrified to look down, as he jumped from rooftop to rooftop across the city. The city lights were beginning to turn on as the sky grew darker. In the distance, she could see the river. A way out . . . a way for the yeti to get to Everest.

"Hurry!" she urged. The sound of the helicopter was growing closer, and she turned to see a Burnish security guard leaning out of the passenger door, aiming a tranquilizer gun at them.

Suddenly, Yi felt the yeti drop between two buildings. The guard took his shot, missing them. The yeti raced through the alleyways until they reached a construction site. He grabbed onto a giant crane as it swung across a huge glass building shaped like a globe. Then he let go and began to slide down the smooth, curved roof.

"Whooooooaaa!" Yi cried.

They stopped at the edge of the glass roof. The river stretched out in front of them, calm and inviting. Yi pointed to the docks.

"Look, down there," she said. "That boat's leaving the city. You have to get on it!"

As soon as she said the words, the helicopter swooped in front of them. Below, a small army of Burnish Industries vehicles surrounded the building. Then, to Yi's surprise, Jin and Peng pulled up, riding on a pink scooter. A pink scooter? And was Peng wearing a helmet with a unicorn face on it? Yi had no idea how they'd gotten any of that stuff, but she was glad to see them. They were the only friendly faces in the crowd.

Jin spotted Yi, too. "There she is!" he cried, pointing.

Nearby, the security captain yelled, "Take the shot!"

Dr. Zara focused on the yeti with her binoculars. "There's a girl with him!"

Jin overheard. *How is she going to get away?* he wondered. If they shot the yeti and he went limp, Yi would go tumbling down with him. . . . Then it hit him. "Wait, wait. What time is it?"

Peng glanced at his watch. "Eight o'clock. Why?"

Then Peng grinned, getting it. "Time for the light show!" he said, at the same time as his cousin. The timing was perfect! The building was one of the city's biggest tourist attractions, and the light show started at the same time every night, every day of the year.

Music began to blare from speakers set up around the building. Colorful lights burst forth from inside the glass globe, shooting rays across the sky.

The light blinded the helicopter, and it jerked sideways. The guard holding the tranquilizer gun was thrown backward into the helicopter, missing his shot.

Dr. Zara squinted up at the building, trying to see the yeti, but the light blinded her, too. Ten minutes later, when the music ended and the lights faded, there was no sign of the yeti on the roof.

"Where are they?" Dr. Zara asked into her headset.

"They're gone!" the helicopter pilot reported.

The security captain next to Dr. Zara called to the other guards. "Come on! Keep searching!"

Jin looked around frantically—and caught a glimpse of Yi and the yeti running toward the docks. He and Peng jumped back onto the scooter and raced after them.

The yeti reached the docks first. Yi gestured

toward a cargo barge preparing to shove off.

"Over there! That one!" she urged the yeti.

They quickly reached the barge.

"You have to get on that boat," she told him.

The yeti looked confused.

"When that boat lands, don't stop. Don't stop until you reach your mountain. Don't stop until you're home, okay? Home." She made a triangle with her hands, like she had before.

Whooooooo! The barge's horn sounded as it started to pull away from the dock. But the yeti didn't move.

"You have to go now," she pleaded with him.

His eyes full of worry, he obeyed Yi and leaped onto the barge. Then he looked around, unsure of what to do.

"Hide!" Yi shouted.

The yeti tried to squeeze between some boxes, but he didn't fit. He pulled a tarp over his head, but it blew off and into the water.

Yi felt a tug on her heartstrings. He looked so helpless!

Jin and Peng pulled up on the scooter and hopped off. They both stared at Yi, concerned.

"Yi, are you okay?" Jin asked.

Yi saw Jin running toward her, then turned to see the barge pulling away. It was clear the yeti would never make it on his own.

"Oh no. No, Yi, don't you dare!" he cried.

She ignored him and sprinted toward the boat. With a mighty leap, she hurled herself off the dock and landed on the deck of the barge.

She smiled at the yeti. "Guess I'm coming with you, huh, Everest?" she said.

The yeti let out a happy hoot! Yi laughed. "I guess you like your new name?"

"Yi, are you crazy?" Jin called from the dock.

Peng pushed past his cousin. "Wait for me, Yi!" he called out.

He raced down the dock and took a mighty leap, just as Yi had. But he came up a few feet short of the barge.

"No, no, no!" he wailed, squeezing his eyes shut.

Everest reached out and caught him in midair. Peng opened his eyes and smiled at him, and Everest smiled back.

Back on the dock, Jin was furious. "Peng, I'm responsible for you! Your mom's going to kill me!"

Jin reluctantly took off and jumped onto the

barge, landing successfully in a puddle of oil. He looked down at his ruined brand new sneakers.

"My babies!" he squeaked, and Peng burst out laughing. To make things worse, Everest was laughing too. "You think this is funny?" Jin exclaimed. "Do you even know how much I paid for these?"

Jin walked up to Yi, who had her back to him as she gazed over the railing of the barge.

"What were you thinking, Yi?" he asked, pacing back and forth. "You have gotten me into so much trouble. I am so mad at you right now. You know what? I can't even talk to you. That's how mad I am."

Yi wasn't really listening. A slight smile crept onto her face as the city became more and more distant.

The money, the postcards, the maps . . . she had been planning a journey for a long time. Maybe this wasn't the journey she had dreamed of, but it was the one she was on. It was strange, and scary . . . but also exciting.

She couldn't wait to see where the journey would take them.

Chapter Five
Blueberries

Over at Burnish Industries, the very angry owner of the company was scolding Dr. Zara and the security captain.

"The unveiling is in one week, Captain," Mr. Burnish snapped. "Now how am I supposed to prove that the yeti exists when I don't have a yeti?"

Suddenly, he jumped out of his chair and stepped up to the top of his desk, using an ice axe as a cane.

"Uhhh . . . . ," the security captain stammered.

"No speaking!" Mr. Burnish bellowed, waving the ice axe in the captain's face. Then he pointed the axe toward the door. "Only leaving!" he yelled.

The captain walked out, hanging his head. Dr. Zara didn't move, but cocked her head to one side and stared at Mr. Burnish with steely eyes. The furry rodent on her shoulder did the same.

Mr. Burnish hopped off his desk and began to pace. "Dr. Zara, what am I going to do?" he wondered. "The science community will be there, the press will be there, the *world* will be there . . . watching with their eyes."

"Mr. Burnish, there are many rare and exotic animals you have collected over the years," Dr. Zara reminded him. "These snakes, for example."

She snapped her fingers and a lab tech wheeled in a glass aquarium filled with sand.

"You are the only one in the world to have a newly born clutch of rare whooping snakes," she said.

Three snakes popped their heads out of the sand. "Whoop! Whoop! Whoop!" they sang.

Mr. Burnish bopped each of them on the head with his ice axe. "Down! Down! Down! Go in your holes, you weird snakes!"

Dr. Zara snatched the axe from his hand. "Sir, please! These creatures are to be respected!"

"Whoop!" agreed the snakes, and they curled up on top of the sand.

Mr. Burnish eyed their spotted scales. "Hmm, they *would* make a lovely belt."

Dr. Zara gasped. "Mr. Burnish, they are one of a kind!"

"A one-of-a-kind whooping belt," Mr. Burnish said with a laugh. "A belt that goes whoop! Do I want that? I don't know."

The doctor waved her hand, and the tech wheeled away the snakes. As they were leaving, one of the lab techs looked worriedly into the aquarium and said quietly to the other tech, "Wait, how many snakes were there supposed to be?"

"Why?" the second tech whispered back. A snake was missing!

"We promised the public a yeti, and nothing else will do! Nothing!" Mr. Burnish insisted, banging his fist on the table. "I don't care if the yeti is dead or alive, I just need him!"

Dr. Zara's face went white with horror.

"Your gerbil is freaking me out," Mr. Burnish said.

"Jerboa!" she corrected him. "Duchess is an albino jerboa and she, too, is one of a kind. Sir, as a zoologist, it is my mission in life to make sure that all animals are protected, especially the rare and exotic ones. That is the *only* reason I agreed to find your yeti."

"And you did!" Mr. Burnish replied. "For a few short days we had one. . . . But I cannot go to the unveiling empty-handed. I will *not* be made a laughing stock again. Not, not, not, not, NOT!"

The security captain returned.

"Uh, there's news, Mr. Burnish," he said.

"News about you leaving?" Mr. Burnish asked.

"A dock worker saw a creature and some kids boarding a cargo barge last night."

Mr. Burnish's eyes lit up. He pushed past the captain and faced Dr. Zara.

"You are the best in your field. Please help me get him back," he pleaded.

Dr. Zara considered this, frowning. "Under one condition," she said finally. "We bring the yeti back *alive.* You have to promise me he won't be harmed."

"Fine, fine, fine, fine, fine," Mr. Burnish said dismissively, and Dr. Zara rolled her eyes. She would take him at his word—for now.

Yi, Peng, Jin, and Everest spent the night on the deck of the barge and managed to remain unseen by the crew as they slept amid cargo boxes. They woke up at sunrise as the barge made its way through the small islands scattered across Qiandao Lake in Zhejiang Province.

Jin stood by the rear railing, talking on his cell phone. "Yeah, Ma. Beijing is . . . great. And the dorms . . . the dorms are clean. Peng? Peng is, uh . . ."

He glanced over at his cousin, whose entire head was stuck in Everest's mouth.

"Look at all of those teeth," Peng marveled. Jin's eyes were wide with horror, but he held it together.

"Uh . . . Peng's fine," Jin told his mother.

Yi motioned to Jin.

"Oh, and Yi came too," Jin said, repeating the story they had worked out. "She's checking out the university."

Peng noticed a wood crate labeled SODA. "Soda? Oh yeah! Mom never lets me have any!"

He opened the crate and—JACKPOT!—it was filled with soda cans. Peng opened up a can and guzzled it down. Everest stared at him, intrigued.

Peng tossed him a can. "Catch!"

Everest bit into it. Foam sprayed into his nostrils, then his eyes lit up as the sugary liquid hit his tongue.

Yi walked over to a pile of coal and picked up a piece. "Hey Everest, come on over here," she said. Everest obeyed, and she crouched down and began to draw on the deck of the barge using the coal.

Jin finished his call and strode over to Yi. "I cannot believe you made me lie to my mother!"

Yi ignored him, concentrating on her drawing. "Okay, Everest, look. First you go over the Yellow Mountain."

She pointed to a mountain she had drawn, and then drew wavy lines next to it.

"Then to the Yangtze River," she said, pointing to the lines. "And that river will take you most of the way to the Himalayas. And finally . . ."

She drew a mountain much larger than the others. "To Mount Everest. This is how you're going to get home."

"Whoa, wait," Jin said. "Mount Everest? That has to be hundreds of miles away."

Peng whizzed by, fueled by soda. "Actually, it's

thousands. Whoooo! I love soda!"

"I just hope he can make it all that way," Yi said. She glanced at the yeti, whose tongue was stuck in the plastic six-pack rings from the soda. He jumped up and down, trying to get loose from it, erasing Yi's map in the process.

"He, um . . . he seems capable," Jin said.

As the sun rose higher in the sky, the barge reached the Qiandao docks, where hundreds of workers waited to unload its cargo.

Peng climbed to the top of the coal pile. "Look at all those people," he remarked. He raised his voice. "Hello!"

"Get down!" Jin snapped, pulling him out of sight.

Yi glanced up at Everest. "Yeah, we should hide."

"How?" Peng asked. "Once we dock, we'll be seen."

She glanced at the huge soda crate. "I think I have an idea. . . ."

They climbed in the crate and secured the top. They waited until they felt a crane lifting the crate, carrying them through the air. Then they felt the crate being set down.

"We'll wait until everyone's gone from the dock,

and then we'll climb out," Yi instructed. "Everest can go on his way, and we'll hop on the next boat back home."

Suddenly, they felt the crate moving again—not up this time, but forward.

"Wait, why are we still moving?" Jin asked.

Yi peered through the slats. "Uh, cause we're not on the dock anymore."

"Wait, what?" Jin asked. He looked outside too, and saw the dock moving farther and farther away from them. They were on a truck, heading into the countryside!

"Noooooooooo!" Jin wailed.

It wasn't the plan, but they couldn't jump from the moving truck. So they waited to see where it would end up. Peng and Everest gulped down more sodas. Yi watched the scenery pass by, miles and miles of rolling hills and tree-lined meadows.

"You know, I have never been out of the city. Wow, I can't believe how beautiful it is out here," she remarked.

"I can't believe I haven't eaten in twenty-four hours," Jin said, crankily. "I'm starving." Then he took a selfie as he frowned sadly.

Peng put down his soda can and made a strange face. "Uh oh. Guys, I gotta go."

"Just hold it," Jin told him.

But then Everest whined and made the same face.

"Oh no. *He's* got to go!" Yi said.

Jin pushed on one side of the crate. "Get me out of here!"

Yi knew they had to take a risk. Nobody wanted to find out what a crate full of yeti pee smelled like.

Yi pushed against the side of the crate with Jin. "Push! Push!"

The crate rocked back and forth. The truck slowed down to take a curve, and the crate tumbled off the truck bed and down into an embankment. It burst open, scattering its passengers—and soda cans—everywhere.

Peng and Everest jumped up and ran into a nearby thicket to relieve themselves.

"Gotta go, gotta go!" Peng wailed.

Yi rubbed her head, and Jin held up his cell phone, searching for a signal.

"Okay, come on, come on," he said. He checked the screen. "One bar? Good enough."

"Good enough for what?" Yi asked.

Jin walked into the thicket, typing on his screen. "Okay, look, the next boat leaves around five, so let's hope that's enough time to find our way back to the dock."

He lowered his phone. "Peng, come on, we're leaving. Peng?"

Jin and Yi entered a clearing and found Peng lying on his back, daydreaming.

"Yes, waiter. I'm ready to order. I'll have some of NaiNai's pork buns . . . with extra pork . . . and a side of pork!"

"All right, get up, Peng," Jin said. "We gotta go!"

Everest's stomach growled. And then he began to hum.

"Why is he making that noise? Is he . . . humming?" Jin asked incredulously.

But Yi recognized the hum—it was the same sound Everest had made when she played her violin. "Shhh, Jin."

Everest's fur began to glow with blue light. Peng sat up. "What's going on? Whoa!"

"What is happening?" Jin asked.

Suddenly . . . *pop!* A blueberry appeared on one of the bushes in the thicket.

Jin's eyes widened. "Is that a . . ."

Yi got a closer look. "A blueberry!"

Everest continued to hum, and hundreds of blueberries popped up on the bushes all around them. Yi, Jin, and Peng stared in silence.

Everest stopped humming and ran over to a cluster of the berries and began to gorge on them.

"Food!" Peng cheered. He joined Everest, popping blueberries into his mouth. Even as he picked them, more kept growing!

"Guys, these are delicious," Peng reported.

Jin leaned over to examine a blueberry that was growing to the size of a basketball.

"This doesn't make any sense," he said.

Pop! The blueberry exploded, splashing juice all over Jin's face and clothes. Yi, Peng, and Everest laughed.

"It's not funny!" Jin cried. He pointed to his sweater. "This is cashmere!"

"Uh, Jin . . ." Yi pointed behind him. He turned to see more berries growing to the size of beach balls. They looked like they were reaching a breaking point.

"Oh," Jin said.

"Everest, do something!" Yi pleaded.

Everest turned and ran as fast as he could, hollering at the top of his lungs.

"Ruuuuuuuuun!" Yi yelled.

They all bolted as the blueberries launched at them from all sides.

"Incoming!" she cried.

One of the blueberries exploded on Peng. Blueberry juice splattered on everyone.

"I'm hit!" he cried, and he fell to the ground. He laughed. "Tell NaiNai's pork buns I love them," he joked.

Everest scooped Peng off the ground and ran away from the thicket, with Yi and Jin behind him. They made it out of the woods just as . . . *boom!*

A blue mushroom cloud shot into the sky.

Chapter Six
Just a Kid

Covered in blueberry juice, Yi, Jin, Peng, and Everest spent the rest of the day moving in the direction of Mount Everest. They stayed off the main road and forged a path through the woods, where the yeti wouldn't be seen.

"Hey Jin, did you get enough to eat?" Peng teased as they walked.

Jin turned toward his cousin, and a giant blueberry slid off his face. "Let's just say I've got blueberries in places where blueberries should never be."

Peng laughed and ran toward the yeti. "Come on, Everest!"

Everest stopped and formed his arms into a hoop, as Peng had taught him to do along the walk. Peng held up a basketball-size blueberry.

"Okay, watch and learn. Bank shot!" He lobbed the blueberry at Everest. It smacked into the yeti's head, ricocheted off, then exploded in Peng's face. Everest burst into laughter.

They had reached a clearing on a grassy knoll, next to a bubbling brook. Yi set down her backpack.

"I'm exhausted," she said.

"What? Why are you stopping?" Jin asked.

"Because in about five minutes we won't be able to see our hands in front of our faces," she told him. "We need to make camp."

"No, that is exactly why we need to keep moving," Jin countered. "Come on, we need to get back to that dock."

Jin turned back to the trail—and saw a dozen pairs of yellow eyes in the distance peering at him from the darkness. A lone wolf howl echoed through the trees. Jin quickly turned around and returned to the others.

". . . first thing in the morning," he said.

"Yes!" Peng cheered.

They washed off in the brook and settled in for the night. Jin made a bed out of leaves and carefully lay down on it. A mosquito landed on his neck and he swatted it away.

Yi fluffed up her backpack to use as a pillow. She stretched out on the green grass, rested her head, and stared up at the sky.

"There are so many," she said.

"Bugs?" Jin asked.

"Stars," Yi replied.

Jin slapped at another mosquito. "How come they're only swarming me?" he wondered.

"Maybe they're *lady*bugs," Yi teased.

Jin scowled. "Not funny."

Peng followed Yi's gaze. "My mom told me that the stars are our ancestors who always watch over us."

Yi smiled. "My mom says that too."

Suddenly, Peng ran up and snatched the backpack from under Yi's head.

"Peng!" Yi shouted.

Peng put the backpack on his head. The placement of the buttons looked a bit like Everest's eyes.

"*Rooooooar!*" Peng stomped around the clearing, pretending to be a yeti.

Jin shook his cell phone. "No, no, no, no, no! Great! No reception. I'm entirely cut off from my social life."

Yi rolled her eyes. "How traumatic."

"Yeah, Yi, it is!" Jin shot back. "Because unlike you, I like having friends. I'm not some kind of a . . ."

"Loner?" Yi finished for him. "Is that what you were going to say? Well, for your info I'm a self-proclaimed loner. There's a difference, okay?"

"Fine, because in the morning, Peng and I are heading back to the city," Jin said. He looked at her questioningly. Would she go with them?

"I can't leave him," Yi said. "You've seen what he can do. He's amazing. He's . . . magical."

"Oh, so now he's a *magical* yeti?" Jin asked. "Do you realize how crazy you sound?"

"Look what happened with the blueberries," Yi pointed out.

"That wasn't him," Jin argued. "That was a natural phenomenon . . . just one that I can't explain yet."

Peng and Everest were playing a new game. Peng pressed his thumb against Everest's massive one.

"One, two, three, four, I declare a thumb war," Peng chanted. "Go!"

Peng didn't stand a chance. Everest pinned down his tiny thumb with one swift move, laughing.

"Hey, you cheated!" Peng protested.

He lightly punched Everest on the arm. Everest punched back. Peng punched harder. Everest punched harder—and Peng went flying.

"Aaaaahhhhhhhh!"

Peng jumped back to his feet and charged Everest, tackling him. The two of them rolled around on the ground.

"Take that!" Peng cried.

"Will you two please just give it a rest?" Jin called out, and then he shook his head. "Oh my gosh, I'm starting to sound like my parents!"

Yi sat up. "That's it! That's why they get along so well. Everest is just a *kid*. He's probably, like, the same age as Peng. Like, nine years old in yeti years!"

As they talked, Peng was using Everest's own paw to slap his face. "Stop hitting yourself! Stop hitting yourself!" Peng chanted.

"There's no way that *giant* thing is a kid," Jin argued.

"Wait, I'll prove it to you," Yi said. She picked up some rocks from the ground. "Everest, come over here!"

The yeti let go of Peng and came over to Yi. She held up a small rock next to Everest's chest and pointed to him.

"This is you," she said, and then she put the rock down on the ground. Then she placed two bigger rocks right behind the little rock while the yeti watched intently. "These are your parents."

"Aw, you have your mother's eyes," Peng told Everest.

The yeti picked up the two big rocks and held them against his chest. Yi saw tears begin to form in his eyes. Yi touched his arm.

"Don't worry. I will make sure you get home," she promised him.

"What are you going to do?" Jin asked. "Take him all the way back to Mount Everest?"

"Maybe I am, Jin," Yi replied. "He needs to get back to his family."

"What about your family?" Jin countered. "Don't they need you too? Always busy, never home. What's that all about, Yi?"

Yi's cheeks turned red with anger. "Don't talk to me about family. You have no idea. NO idea. Your life is sooooo easy, Jin! Do you even want to be a doctor, or do you just think you'll look good in a white lab coat?"

Loud snores interrupted their argument. They looked to see Peng leaning against Everest's furry body. Both of them were fast asleep.

"I don't care if you think I'm crazy," Yi said. She lay back down on the grass, with her back to Jin this time. Jin lay down on his pile of leaves and turned his back to her, too.

Clutching her violin, Yi tried her best to fall asleep.

She—and Everest—had a long journey ahead, with or without Jin's help.

Chapter Seven
Over the Yellow Mountain

Exhausted, Yi fell into a deep sleep. The morning sun woke her up. Everest was already awake, but Jin and Peng were both snoring peacefully, so she picked up her violin, and she and Everest walked away from the camp. She sat on a rock near the brook and played a melody to Everest and the rising sun.

Eyes closed, lost in the music, she played until she heard a twig snap nearby. Her eyes flew open to see Peng and Jin watching her.

"Wait, don't stop," Peng said. "It's really good."

Yi quickly put the violin back in its case.

Peng pressed her. "Your NaiNai said you stopped playing since your dad died."

"Peng!" Jin interrupted him.

"It's okay, Jin, really," Yi replied. Peng was just a kid. She knew he wasn't trying to make her feel bad.

"Was this your dad's violin?" Peng asked, touching the case.

Yi nodded. "Mm-hmm."

"You know, I really liked your dad," the boy said sincerely.

"Thanks, Peng," Yi said with an awkward smile.

Jin stepped between them and held up his phone. "Well, we'd better head out if we're going to make it to the Yangtze River."

Yi brightened. "You're coming?"

"Yeah!" Jin said. "I checked and Da He Village has boats leaving for the city every hour."

Yi's smile dropped. "Okay, well when we get there, you and Peng can take a boat back, but I'm going to take Everest home."

Everest walked over to Yi and touched his forehead to hers, and she knew he was grateful. Jin just sighed as the four of them headed out toward their next destination, the Yangtze River.

Back at Qiandao docks, a large boat had just dropped anchor. It carried a small RV and three black SUVs. One of the vehicles towed a platform with a large iron cage on top.

Mr. Burnish, Dr. Zara, and the security captain stepped off the boat, followed by a small troop of security guards. Dr. Zara began questioning the dock workers whether they'd recently seen a teenage girl with a strange beast.

One of the dock workers pointed to a barge. "Well, that pulled in yesterday morning, but we've unloaded all of the cargo and didn't find anyone."

"Would you mind if we search it again?" Dr. Zara asked.

The dock worker agreed, and Dr. Zara led the security force in a sweeping search of the barge. The guards didn't find anything, but Dr. Zara's sharp eyes spotted some sooty footprints—enormous, yeti footprints—on the back deck. She followed them to a trail of empty soda cans that led to the rail of the barge.

Mr. Burnish approached her and noticed the prints too. "The yeti? He was here?"

"Yes, and it looks like he fancies soda," she replied.

They ordered everyone into the vehicles and made their way onto the road. Dr. Zara stood on the front grill of the transporter as it followed the trail of empty soda cans. She grinned. They might just find the yeti yet!

They barreled down the country road for miles, and the empty cans got farther and farther apart. Just when Dr. Zara thought the trail might end, she spotted the big broken crate down the embankment.

"Stop!" she yelled.

The convoy came to a screeching halt. A whooping snake popped up in the back seat of the transporter. "Whoop!" Mr. Burnish and the security captain looked at each other.

"What was that?" asked the captain. Dr. Zara examined the crate while the guards swept the area. After about twenty minutes, the security captain circled back.

"Sorry, Doctor," he told her. "No sign of them anywhere."

Dr. Zara frowned, knowing she had to break the news to Mr. Burnish.

"Sir, the yeti has disappeared," she began.

Mr. Burnish looked around. "It's been so long since I've been out in nature," he said wistfully.

"Sir, if we—"

He touched the weeping willow next to him. "Look at this tree. It's a wonderful tree. Look at the colors. I love this tree!"

He pointed his ice axe at one of the guards. "You there. Chop it down and put it in a bag, will you? I want it in my penthouse."

"Right away, sir," the guard replied, and he ran off to find a chainsaw.

Dr. Zara raised her voice. "Mr. Burnish!"

He turned. "Right! What is it?"

"We should divide the team and cover some ground," she told him, as the guard returned with a chainsaw and began to rev it up.

Mr. Burnish nodded. "Captain, let's fan out!" he boomed.

"Yes sir!" the security captain replied, as the willow tree crashed to the ground.

Not too far away, Yi, Jin, Peng, and Everest made their way up a grassy hill while Jin studied a map on his phone.

"On the map, the village is only, like, an inch

away," he said. "That can't be that far."

"It must be on the other side of—" Yi reached the top of the hill and stopped. A tall, jagged mountain rose up in front of them. Mist swirled around the top, and ancient stairs wove a twisting pathway to the peak.

"The Yellow Mountain. Wow," she said.

Everest and Peng gazed up at it in awe. Jin, on the other hand, looked horrified.

"Wait . . . we are *not* going over that," he said.

Peng broke into a run. "Come on, Everest. I'll race you!"

The boy and the yeti raced for the stairs. Yi followed them, as did Jin, with a reluctant sigh. Peng might have been full of energy at the start, but he fizzled out before they were halfway up the mountain. Everest dragged Peng behind him.

They stopped at an overlook covered with fuzzy dandelions. Peng plucked one.

"Ooh, Everest, look. Make a wish," he said.

Everest took it from Peng's hand and gobbled it down.

"No, no, no, they're for wishing," Peng told him, as Yi and Jin caught up to them, puffing and panting.

Peng picked another dandelion and closed his eyes. "I wish I was a basketball superstar," he said.

He blew on the flower, and the fluffy dandelion seeds separated and floated through the air. Yi smiled and picked a dandelion.

Peng ran to the edge of the overlook, cupped his hands around his mouth, and called out in an announcer's voice, "Starting in the championship game—the Mighty Peng!"

At that moment, a drone rose up from below and stopped in front of Peng.

"Wait, is that a drone?" Peng wondered. "Cool!"

Another drone appeared and buzzed around Everest's head. Red lights lit up and the drone made a beeping sound. Then four more drones rose up, surrounding them all.

"Okay, not so cool. Not so cool!" Peng cried.

Yi and Jin peered over the ledge and spotted a black SUV, and some Burnish Industries security guards.

"Oh no. It's those guys from the city," Yi said.

"I told you this was a crazy idea," Jin said. "What now?"

Yi looked around, frowning. "I have no idea. I wish there was a way out of here."

Everest looked at Yi. Then he looked at the drone, then back at Yi. He started to hum. The dandelion in Yi's hand began to grow larger and larger.

"What's going on?" Jin asked, as the dandelion grew as tall as Yi, with a flower bigger than her head.

A gust of wind blew, catching the flower. Yi's feet lifted off the ground.

"Yi, let go of that! It's dangerous!" Jin yelled.

Yi looked at the yeti. "Everest, are you sure about this?"

The dandelion had grown even larger. Everest grabbed Peng with one arm and grabbed the thick stem with the other as the dandelion rose higher into the sky.

"No, Peng. Get down from there right now!" Jin demanded.

Peng held out his hand. "Jin, jump!"

Jin climbed the stairs as fast as he could, as the giant dandelion floated higher. The drones followed him.

"Jump!" Yi urged Jin.

"No, get down here!" Jin shouted back.

He jumped up and tried to reach Peng's hand, but couldn't make contact. He watched helplessly as they floated away.

"Can you hear me? Meet me in that village by the river!" Jin called out.

"We'll be there!" Yi replied.

"And take care of Peng!" Jin added.

A gust of wind swept up, sending the dandelion flying higher into the sky and away from Jin. Then a drone crashed into the dandelion, knocking off fluff and pushing them off course.

"Wait! Wait, where are we going?" Yi cried.

Whoosh! The giant dandelion was swallowed by clouds. As Jin watched them go, he was suddenly surrounded by drones.

Chapter Eight
Lost in the Desert

A hungry family of four tortoises (two adults and two babies) approached a blade of grass in a vast desert of red clay that stretched out as far as the eye could see. Suddenly Yi, Peng, and Everest descended from the sky, screaming as the giant dandelion emerged from a bank of clouds. The fluffy seeds began to break off one by one, and the dandelion rapily descended toward the ground. The terrified tortoises disappeared into their shells.

"Brace yourselves!" Yi yelled.

Boom! A cloud of dust filled the air as they landed in the desert. The remaining fluffy dandelion seeds cushioned their fall. The blade of grass was gone. The four turtles lay on the ground pulled into their shells, looking like brown rocks.

"Everest! I'm over here!" Peng called out as Everest looked around, confused. "No! Over here!" Everest spun around. Peng clung to Everest's back. He slid off onto the sand, landing facedown. "I'm okay!" Peng announced good-naturedly, standing up and brushing dust off of his clothes.

"That was amazing, Everest," Yi said. "You saved us, and now we're . . . Where are we?"

Peng frowned. "A long way from Jin."

"Well, that's his fault. He should've jumped! I mean, why doesn't he ever just JUMP?!" Yi exclaimed with annoyance.

"Well, he jumped on that boat back in the city. That's what got him on this trip in the first place," Peng pointed out.

"Yeah, but that's because he was worried about you. You're his family," Yi replied.

"He thinks of you as family too," Peng said.

Everest scooped up two big rocks and a small one and held them out to Yi and cooed. Yi knew he meant "family."

The "rocks" suddenly popped their tortoise heads out, nearly scaring Everest to death. Peng laughed and noticed the other baby tortoise on the ground.

"Hey, little turtle," Peng said, as he picked it up and held it out to Everest as if it were a young Yi.

"Everest, Jin said Yi was like his little sister when they were kids." Peng waved the "Yi" tortoise in the air with a flourish. "She was always doing something CRAZY that would get her into trouble. So he watched out for her." He placed the baby "Yi" turtle into Everest's hands next to the baby "Jin" turtle. The two babies touched heads as Peng looked over at Yi and said, "He still does."

Yi should have been comforted by Peng's story, but it only gave her an ache in her heart, one she didn't really understand. She changed the subject.

"I . . . I think we should get going," she said as she gazed at the vast, windy desert around them. She had no idea which way to go, or how far away from civilization they were. But she had to be strong for the kids, even if one of the kids was big and hairy and magical.

"But don't worry! I can get us out of here," she said, trying to sound confident. "Let's go."

The wind picked up as they headed out across the desert, leaving the tortoises behind to feast on the giant dandelion stem. Yi held her head high. No one would ever know how uncertain she felt.

Chapter Nine
Jin and the Villains

Back at the Yellow Mountain, Jin reached the Burnish Industries convoy at the bottom of the steps. The security guards surrounded him, as Dr. Zara approached him.

"I hope you're not hurt," she said. "Let me introduce myself. I'm Dr. Zara."

"I know who you are!" Jin blurted out.

"You do?" she asked.

"Yeah." He took a deep breath. "You're the *bad guys*."

Duchess popped out of Dr. Zara's hair and moved to her shoulder.

Jin jumped back. "Whoa! Your gerbil is freaking me out!"

Mr. Burnish turned to the security captain. "A boy who knows his gerbils. I like him."

"Bad?" Dr. Zara asked Jin. "You've got this all wrong. That wild beast is unpredictable, even dangerous. We were trying to *rescue* your friend when the yeti kidnapped her."

"He did kidnap her," Jin admitted. His mind was spinning. He had seen Everest pick up Yi and carry her off. And those weird powers of his . . . that yeti was definitely unpredictable.

Impatient, Mr. Burnish poked Jin in the chest with the tip of his ice axe.

"Listen, I own that yeti," he said. "He is *my* yeti. I want my yeti back! Right? Just nod."

"Mr. Burnish, please," Dr. Zara said.

She gave Mr. Burnish a stern look as she took Jin aside.

"I just need to find my cousin and my friend, and get them back to the city in one piece," Jin told her.

Dr. Zara lowered her voice. "I can get all of you back to the city. But the only way I can help your friends is if I know where they are. Do you know?"

Jin shook his head. He had no idea where that giant flower had carried them. Poor Peng could be anywhere, and in danger, and Jin believed it was all his fault.

"That yeti is the pinnacle of my research." Dr. Zara's confidence faded and she seemed vulnerable. "I really need him back."

Jin eyed the doctor and almost felt sorry for her.

"I don't know where they are," he said. "But I do know where they will be."

Dr. Zara smiled at him. "Excellent. Now, you see, we can help each other."

She led Jin into one of the SUVs and then spoke with Mr. Burnish and the security captain. Jin relaxed into the soft, comfortable seat, exhausted. Then they took off into the countryside, headed toward the village along the Yangtze.

When night fell, they made camp in a clearing. The guards set up tents and built a roaring bonfire. Jin and Mr. Burnish sat outside the RV, a luxury vehicle that looked like a small apartment. Jin contentedly sipped on steaming cocoa as Mr. Burnish regaled him with his experience in the Himalayas.

"And suddenly I saw it—a yeti!" Mr. Burnish went on. "A real yeti. Cold eyes staring. It was going to kill me. I swung my axe—"

He recreated the moment by swinging his ice axe, and Jin had to duck.

"—and it was gone. No footprints. Nothing."

Mr. Burnish looked down at the axe, remembering.

"I rushed back to tell the world what had happened, but without proof, they laughed at me," he said. He pointed to himself. "They laughed at me."

"And you spent all these years trying to get your proof?" Jin asked.

Mr. Burnish nodded. He turned his gaze toward the starry sky. "I'm so used to looking down on the world," he said. "It's amazing how small one feels just by looking up."

Jin looked up at the sky, and for an instant, he knew just what Mr. Burnish meant.

Dr. Zara quickly approached them. "Mr. Burnish, we need to get an early start," she said. "We'll catch up to that yeti tomorrow, thanks to Jin."

Jin cringed at the reminder that he had betrayed Yi. *But I'm doing it for Peng,* he told himself. *For all of us! Yi doesn't know what she's getting into.*

He nodded to the adults and headed inside the RV. Mr. Burnish stood up and smiled at Duchess, who was perched, as usual, on Dr. Zara's shoulder. He tickled the furry creature under the chin.

"Duchess, is that your name?" he asked. "You're kind of cute, you know, in your own ugly, beady-eyed kind of way."

He turned and went inside the vehicle, and Dr. Zara's eyes widened in shock.

Meanwhile, Jin sank into the comfy mattress in the guest room of the RV and gave a contented sigh. This was so much better than a bunch of leaves, he thought. And no mosquitoes!

Still, he couldn't sleep. He stared at the ceiling worrying about Peng and Yi . . . and Everest.

He's just a kid! Yi had said about Everest. The more Jin thought about it, the more he felt Yi was right. A kid who would probably be terrified by Mr. Burnish's ice axe . . .

Restless, Jin got up and walked outside. He needed to think. But above the sound of the guards snoring in their tents, he heard intense whispers. Jin decided to investigate. He snuck over to one of the SUVs and peeked out from behind it. In the moonlight, he saw Dr. Zara talking to the security captain.

"You're cute in your own ugly, beady-eyed kind of way," she said, mocking Mr. Burnish. "I tell you, he's going soft!"

Jin stifled a gasp. Dr. Zara had dropped her fancy British accent. She sounded American! But why would she need to fake an accent?

Dr. Zara tossed a stun gun to the security captain.

"I thought we had to keep the yeti alive," the captain said, wrinkling his bushy brows.

"The buyer won't pay us unless he's still breathing, but if he's a little banged up, who cares?" Dr. Zara said coldly. "They're just going to chop him up into little pieces for their experiments, anyway."

"And what do we do with the kids?" the captain asked.

She looked at him with steely eyes. "Well, if you want your ten percent, you'll get rid of them! For good!"

Jin's mouth opened in shock, and he realized he had trusted the wrong person! She was truly evil!

"Oh, and get rid of this rodent I've been carrying around," she continued. "Do you know how hard it is to keep up this British animal lover act? I'm done!"

"Duchess? But she's a one-of-a-kind albino jerboa," the captain said. He playfully jingled his keys in front of Duchess, and she grabbed them with her teeth.

"She's just a rat, you idiot!" Dr. Zara fumed. She flung Duchess off her shoulder and onto the grass right next to Jin.

The captain's keys still dangled from her mouth. Jin quietly picked her up and crept away.

First, he cracked open the door of the RV and placed Duchess inside with Mr. Burnish.

"I think you're better off with this guy," he whispered.

Then he examined the keys. "All right, let's see. SUV? Too loud. Transporter? No. What's this one?"

He grinned and looked around the camp to see a chrome motorcycle glistening in the moonlight.

"Sweet!" he whispered.

He sat on the bike, turned the key in the ignition, and the engine purred. Then he checked his hair in the mirror and quietly said to himself, "Looking good, Jin! Thanks, Jin!" Choking on the throttle, he gunned it. The bike zoomed forward without him!

Wham! The motorcycle slammed into a tree. At

first, Jin just stood there in shock. But soon, adrenaline pumped through his body. He didn't need a motorcycle. He would get to Peng and the others before the bad guys did, somehow, some way!

Determined, he ripped the sleeve off his designer shirt and tied it around his head. Then he let out a cry and plunged into the woods.

He emerged in a small fishing village. Perfect! The fishermen didn't bat an eye at his tattered clothes or dirt-streaked face.

"Can I get a lift to Da He Village?" he asked one person after another. Nobody was willing, but one woman pointed to his phone.

"Your phone for my boat."

"No, anything but the phone!" Jin wailed. But he didn't have anything else to trade.

Dr. Zara's voice echoed in his head. *Get rid of them! For good!*

Jin sighed and handed over the phone. Then he grabbed the rope attached to the boat and dragged it toward the water.

"Enjoy!" he called out sarcastically.

The woman happily took a selfie as Jin sailed off into the night.

Chapter Ten
Be the Koi Fish

While Jin had camped out with the villains, Yi, Peng, and Everest walked across the desert. They walked, and walked, and walked until they were exhausted. They finally reached a large grove of trees, and the three of them flopped onto the hard ground near a rippling stream.

"I can't feel my feet," Peng groaned.

Everest moaned in agreement.

"What was I thinking?" Yi wondered out loud. "We are completely lost. Everest is nowhere near his mountain, and for all we know, Jin could be in trouble right now. I hate this. And it's all my fault!"

Peng and Everest looked at her.

"Jin said this trip was a crazy idea," she continued. "And I don't know, maybe he's right. But we could sure use him now."

"And the map on his cell phone," Peng agreed.

Sploosh! At that moment, a large koi fish leaped out of the water and smacked Everest in the face. Everest yelped and jumped behind Yi.

"It's okay, Everest. It's a koi fish," she assured him.

Peng looked down into the stream. *Sploosh! Sploosh!* More fish jumped out of the water as they made their way upstream.

"Why are they swimming against the current?" he asked.

"Well, they're actually trying to get back home," Yi explained.

Excited and curious, Everest leaned over and watched the fish swim upstream. Then he reached in, pulled a fish out of the water, and tried to talk to it. The fish slapped him in the face and fell to the ground. Yi scooped it up.

"Yeah. Let's put him back," Yi said as she gently placed the fish in the water.

"Do you think he'll make it? All the way home, I mean," Peng asked as he watched the fish struggle up the river.

Yi nodded. "Well, he's sure gonna try. You know these fish are 'the symbol of perseverance.'"

"What?" Peng asked.

"It's just something my mom told me,"she answered. "It means that when things get really tough, they never give up. . . ."

Her face suddenly lit up as her mother's words truly inspired her. "They never give up!"

Yi stood up. "You know what, you guys? We have to keep going. Come on!" As they walked off, Yi turned to see Everest with another fish. "Everest, put the fish back," she said. When he placed the fish carefully on the ground, she reminded him. "In the water!" Everest solemnly put the fish back in the water, and it swam off.

They followed the stream through the grove. Walking under the shade of the trees was better than being in the desert, at least, but the grove seemed to have no end. As the sun rose, they finally emerged from the grove having walked all through the night.

"Be the koi fish. Be the koi fish," Peng, who was

half asleep, chanted while moving his arms like a swimmer.

"That's it, Peng," Yi coached. "You're doing great."

Whoot! A train whistle blew in the distance.

"What was that?" Yi asked. "Come on!"

"Yay! No more swimming!" Peng cheered.

They raced ahead and stopped at a cliff's edge. In the valley below, they saw a train speeding toward them through the lush countryside. They all smiled.

"But how can we get on it if it doesn't stop?" Peng wondered.

Yi turned to Everest. "Any ideas?"

Everest hummed. He glowed. The fall leaves on the ground whirled up into a swirling tornado. The leaves picked up Everest, Peng, and Yi.

Whoosh! They floated above the ground as the train approached. The train whizzed past, but the leaves spun faster.

Whoosh! They carried Everest, Peng, and Yi to the open door of one of the boxcars and dropped them inside. Then the leaf tornado exploded, sending leaves flying everywhere.

Once they caught their breath, the three of them

relaxed among the cargo boxes in the train car.

"Now this is the way to travel!" Peng said, leaning back with his hands behind his head.

Everest hooted in agreement.

"You know, Everest, I can't figure you out," Yi said. "I mean, how do you do that?"

"Maybe it's his gift, like when you play the violin," Peng guessed. "Or when I play basketball. Everest talks to nature."

Yi smiled. "Now that *is* a gift!"

They enjoyed the train ride as they wound their way through the countryside. Luckily, the train stopped at Da He—the village on the Yangtze River where Jin had said they should meet.

Da He was a large fishing village. They cautiously made their way through the village, using the narrow alleys between buildings in order to keep Everest out of sight. The main street was crowded with people shopping in the open-air market. Past that, along the water's edge, fishing boats bobbed up and down in a tangled row.

"Do you see Jin?" Peng asked.

"Through that mob? Are you kidding me?" Yi asked. "We both need to look for him."

"What about Everest?" Peng asked.

Yi thought. They couldn't leave Everest behind by himself. But how could he get through the crowd without being noticed?

Then a man came down the street, moving a herd of big, furry yaks. Their shaggy, dark brown fur hung down almost to their feet. Each one had a pair of curved horns.

Everest could *almost* pass for a yak if you weren't looking too closely, but his fur was white and he had no horns. She scanned the alleyway and her eyes stopped at a pile of junk: crab pots, a length of rope, fishing nets, and a rusty bicycle.

She pried the handlebars off the bike. "Peng, grab all of that rope."

Ten minutes later, the three of them made their way through the marketplace. Rope and fishing nets covered Everest, looking a bit like brown fur. The handlebars stood in for horns. It was a ridiculous disguise, but it seemed to be working. Peng rode on his back, and Yi walked in front of them.

"Can you see anything?" she asked Peng, who had a good view of the crowd from his perch.

Then Peng spotted a guy in jeans and a plaid

shirt. "There he is!" Peng cried. "Jin, Jin!"

But Jin was moving too fast. "We're going to lose him," Peng said.

"I'll run ahead. Stay there . . . blend in," Yi instructed.

She raced into the crowd. Then she saw Jin. She pushed her way through the villagers until she caught up to him by the river.

"Jin!" She grabbed him by the shoulder and spun him around. A toothless old man smiled at her.

Yi jumped back. "Whoa! Sorry!"

She turned to head back to Peng and Everest— and saw the Burnish Industries RV driving slowly toward the village.

Heart pounding, she pushed through the crowd again, but it was dense. She caught a glimpse of Peng and Everest, stuck in the middle of the yak herd. The Burnish security guards were gaining on them from all sides. Yi couldn't reach them in time!

"No!" she yelled.

"Need a ride?" a voice called from the river.

Yi turned to see the real Jin pulling up to the shore in an old boat. His hair was a tangled mess, and his shirt only had one sleeve, but it was definitely Jin.

"You showed up!" she cried happily as she jumped into the boat.

"Of course I did," Jin said. "Wait, where's Peng?"

Yi's head snapped toward the yak herd. Jin's eyes widened at the sight of the men closing in on his cousin.

Peng looked left and right. He was surrounded. He had to break through the herd. But how?

Then he grinned and talked in his sports announcer voice. "Coming in at four-foot-ten and ready to take the game, the Mighty Peng! High five!"

Smack! Peng whacked the butt of the nearest yak.

Smack! Smack! Smack! He whacked every yak he could reach. The startled yaks stampeded in all directions away from Everest, barreling toward the Burnish guards.

"Whoo!" Peng cheered.

"Everest! Peng! Come on!" shouted Yi and Jin as their boat headed down the river toward Peng and Everest.

The boy and the yeti raced to the boat and jumped in with Yi and Jin.

"Good to see you, cuz," Jin said as he revved the tiny outboard motor. The boat zipped upstream, away from the village.

Inside the RV, Mr. Burnish, Dr. Zara, and the security captain watched the boat motor up the river and out of sight.

"Captain, don't you dare let them get away!" Mr. Burnish barked.

"Hold on," the captain replied. "This little lady has a few tricks up her sleeve."

He stepped on the gas, and the RV charged toward the river. Villagers leaped out of the way as it launched off the bank. The captain flipped a switch on the dashboard, and a rubber ring inflated around the vehicle as it flew toward the water.

Splash! The RV landed in the river. Yi and Jin heard the noise and looked back to see the RV gaining on them.

"Go faster!" Yi urged.

"I'm trying!" Jin shot back, but the tiny motor on the boat couldn't compare with the powerful RV.

"Everest, do something!" Yi pleaded.

The yeti began to hum.

"Hurry!" she yelled.

The water around their little boat began to glow, and suddenly the boat picked up speed. The water pushed them away from the RV.

"It's working!" Yi cheered.

Peng had his eyes facing front. The river was about to take a sharp right turn.

"Oh no," he said. "Guys!"

Jin and Yi spotted the danger. "Turn! Turn! Turn!"

They were too late. The boat hit the shoreline and plunged straight into a field of yellow flowers. Everest hummed, and the flowers began to rise and ripple like ocean waves.

Behind them, the RV hit the shore so hard that it tumbled over onto its side. But the little boat kept going across the field, carving through the waves of flowers as if floating on water.

"Whoa, this is amazing!" Yi exclaimed.

Jin clung to the boat, his knuckles white. "This is impossible."

Peng grinned. "Come on, Everest. Make it go bigger!"

Everest hummed louder, and the waves of yellow flowers became larger. Peng stood up and raised his arms as if he were on a roller coaster.

"Higher!"

The waves became the size of tidal waves. Now Yi looked as pale as Jin. The boat crested a huge wave . . .

and Peng lost his balance. He tumbled overboard!

"Slow down!" Yi yelled to Everest.

Everest stopped humming and looked around. The wave dropped, and the boat disappeared into an ocean of flowers.

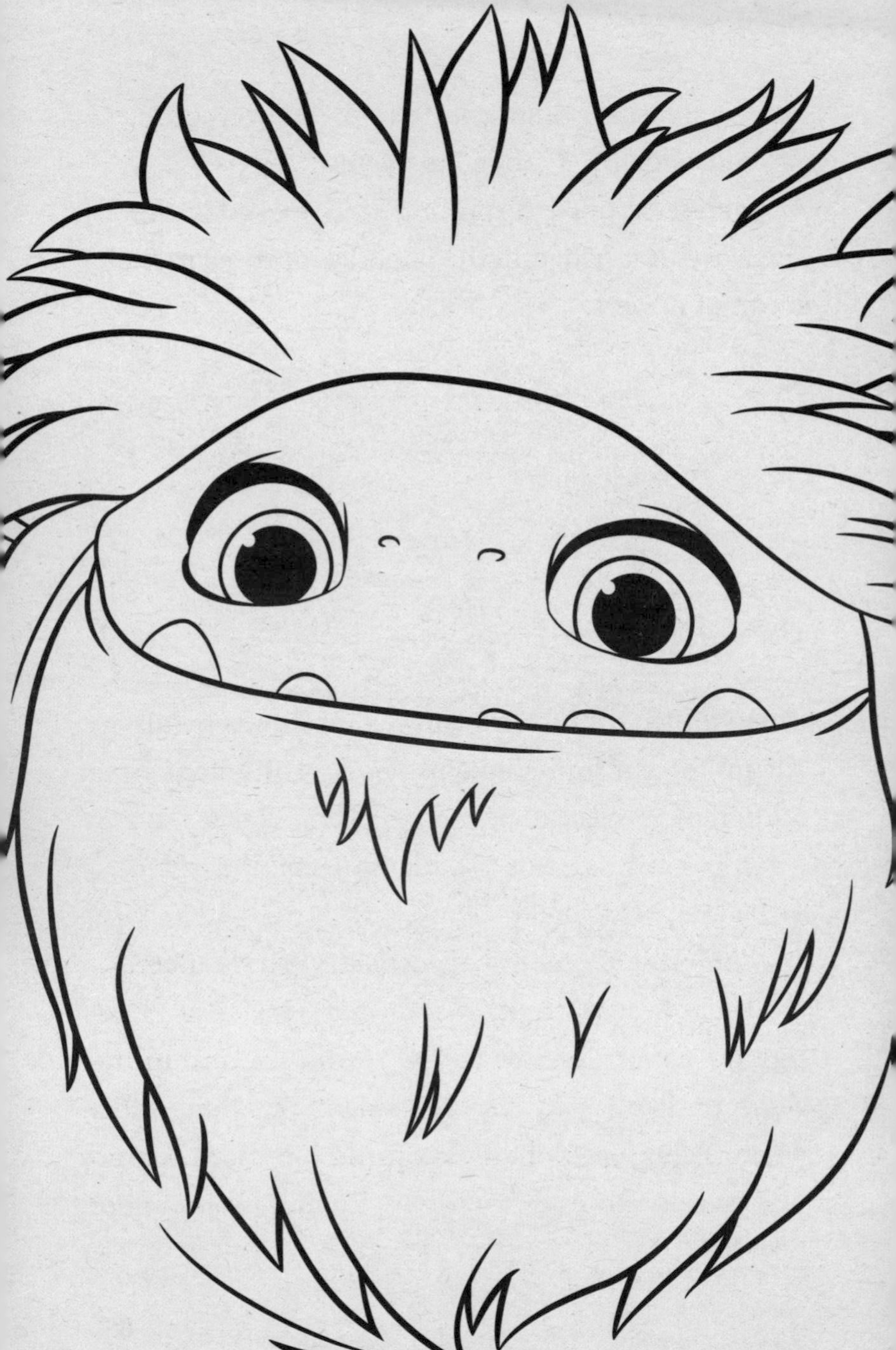

Chapter Eleven
Broken Strings

They landed on a thick, soft bed of flower petals. Yi sat up, dazed and shaken. Pieces of the boat were scattered all around. Jin had landed a few feet away from Yi, but there was no sign of Peng or Everest.

"Peng!" Yi yelled.

Panicked, Jin scanned the field. "Where is he?"

Then Everest appeared at the top of a ridge, motioning for them to come. Yi and Jin ran up the ridge and followed the yeti down the other side, where Peng lay motionless on the ground. Looking like he was about to cry, Everest knelt by Peng's side.

"Peng!" Jin cried. He gently rolled his cousin's body so the boy was face up. Peng's eyes opened. He sat up and made a gagging noise, then barfed up a shower of tiny yellow flowers. Then Everest started to gag too.

"Oh no!" Yi said.

"Oh no!" Jin cried. "Everest, hold it in!"

BLAAAAAH! Everest projectile vomited yellow canola flowers all over Jin!

"Oh Jin, you've got canola flowers in places canola flowers should NEVER be," Yi said with a grin.

Just then Everest let out a worried yelp. Yi followed his gaze to her violin case, which had fallen out of her backpack and landed in the grass.

"NO!!" wailed Yi.

"Oh no!" Peng gasped, horrified.

The postcards were scattered across the ground. Her violin had fallen out, and its neck was cracked and every string was broken.

Everest cooed, trying to comfort her, but Yi was beyond comfort. As Jin called out to her, she ran, not stopping until she reached the cover of a bamboo grove. Then she sat down on a big rock and stared at the ground, trying to process what had just happened.

Jin approached her. "You okay?"

"Yeah." She took a shaky breath. "That violin meant everything to me," she said. "When we were little, you know my dad used to play all the time. But every night when he was tucking me in, he would play this one song just for me. And, I don't know, it made me feel like everything was gonna be okay."

Jin listened. He thought he knew Yi pretty well, but this was something he'd never heard.

"Yi, I'm sorry for what I said . . . that you were too busy and never home," he apologized. "I didn't mean it."

Yi shook her head. "No, you were right. I know I keep busy. I just . . . I don't know why! Maybe it's so I don't really have time to think about him or miss him. I mean, I haven't even cried yet, Jin! My family, we're all so distant," Yi went on. "And I don't know what to do."

"Well, are you sure they're the ones who are distant?" he asked gently.

Yi thought about that. Mom and NaiNai were always there for her, always trying to reach out. Could it be that she was the one pulling away from them?

"But you were right about me, too," Jin confessed. "I hate to admit it, but that thought about looking good in the white doctor's coat? It did cross my mind. I'm a horrible, horrible person."

Yi hiccuped with laughter. "Yeah, you are the worst."

"I really am!" Jin smiled at her but then quickly grew serious. "Yi, listen. If these people find Everest, we're all in danger."

"Do they know where I'm taking him?" Yi asked with alarm.

Mr. Burnish, Dr. Zara, and the security captain walked into Da He Village, which was a mess after the yak stampede. The Burnish Industries vehicles were mostly wrecked.

"They're headed for the Himalayas, Mr. Burnish," Dr. Zara said, using her fake British accent once again. "And the yeti's powers will grow even stronger the closer they get to those mountains. But there's still one more chance to capture your yeti. At the foothills of those mountains there's a bridge. It's the last threshold. Once the yeti crosses it, he'll blend in and disappear. We will never find him again."

Mr. Burnish nodded. "I've never seen powers like those before. It's intimidating."

"Stay the course, sir," Dr. Zara told him. "After this, no one will *ever* laugh at you again."

"You're right," Mr. Burnish agreed. "Captain, we are going to need reinforcements. Lots of reinforcements!"

The security captain saluted him. "Yes sir!"

Mr. Burnish walked away, and the captain leaned in to Dr. Zara.

"What do those powers mean for us?" he whispered.

Dr. Zara's eyes narrowed, and she answered him in her American accent. "That yeti's price tag just doubled!"

The security captain turned to the guards who were searching for something near the wrecked transporter. "Hey, you guys, did you find that thing?" he asked.

"We're working on it!" said one of the guards.

The missing whooping snake popped up from behind one of the transporter's wheels. *Whoop!*

"There it is!" said one of the guards.

And then, from another location, *Whoop!*

"There it is!" said another one of the guards.

And finally, *Whoop!*

"There it IS!" said a third guard as he executed a little dance step.

"*Really*, Dave?" said the security captain.

Chapter Twelve
The Buddha's Tears

Peng ran up to Yi and Jin when they emerged from the bamboo grove. "Come on! Come quickly!"

Yi sprinted ahead. "Everest! You okay?"

Everest held out the violin. Its neck was no longer broken, and it was strung with shimmering white strings. Yi's eyes widened. "Is that . . . ?"

"Yeti hair? Yup!" Peng confirmed.

Everest made a cooing sound.

"See? It's as good as new," Peng said.

Yi hugged Everest tightly. Then she pulled back and looked into his blue eyes.

"No. It's better than new," she said.

As she put the violin back in its case, Peng picked up the scattered postcards.

"Hey, when did you buy these?" he asked, as he looked through them.

"Oh, I didn't buy them," Yi replied. "They were my dad's. He kept postcards of all the places he wanted to take us some day, the whole family."

"Yi, these are all of the places we've been!" Peng said. Yi grabbed the postcards from him and flipped through them.

"No way. How is this possible?" She took the postcards from him, and her eyes widened. There was Qiandao Lake with all of its islands. The big red desert they had walked through—that was the Gobi Desert. The fields of yellow flowers—those were the famous canola fields of Yunnan Province.

She felt weak in the knees and sank down next to her violin case. Jin looked at the postcards and shook his head in disbelief.

"That can't be," he said.

Yi looked at the postcards. "We've been to all of them but one."

Everest laid a final postcard on the stack Yi was

holding. The postcard showed an image of a statue of a seated Buddha carved into the mountains. At two hundred thirty-three feet tall, it towered over the land like a skyscraper. Everest pointed to the sky. The clouds behind him parted, revealing the Leshan Buddha in the distance.

"The Leshan Buddha," Yi said. "This is the place my dad wanted me to see the most." She stared out in disbelief at the statue in the distance. "This is incredible!" She slowly turned to look at Everest. "You brought me here, didn't you?" she asked him quietly. Everest just smiled and looked back at the Buddha.

Peng's mouth dropped open. "Whoa."

"Impossible," Jin said.

But it was real. They walked to the Buddha, reaching it by late afternoon. When they arrived, they stood at its base and stared up at it in awe.

The statue had been carved entirely from the stone of the mountains. The Buddha's hands rested on his knees as he sat, staring calmly into the distance. Yi wanted to get a closer look at that face. One by one, they climbed up the Buddha's leg. Yi stopped on the Buddha's hand.

"Wow, I wish my dad were here to see this," she

said, gazing up at the statue's amazing face.

Everest nudged her violin toward her. Yi took it out of its case and looked at the photo of her dad smiling, and a feeling of peace washed over her.

She held her violin high and began to play the song her dad used to play for her. The song that let Yi know everything was going to be okay. Now, she played the song for her dad.

The music rang through the air, beautiful and sweet. As she played, the strings began to glow with a bluish light. A single tear fell from Yi's cheek, and when it hit the Buddha's hand, a white flower bloomed from the stone.

As Yi played, raindrops began to softly fall from the sky, streaming down from the Buddha's face as if nature were grieving along with Yi. As each raindrop hit the ground, a white flower sprouted. The flowers bloomed along the Buddha's shoulders and down his legs. They bloomed on the surrounding mountains nestling the statue, and they bloomed on the ground below.

She finished the song, and the rain stopped. The clouds parted. She opened her eyes and looked around, stunned, at the white blanket of beauty that surrounded them all.

"It's beautiful," she said. "Thank you, Everest."

Everest shook his head and snorted.

"You did that!" Peng told Yi. "You!"

"I did that?" Yi stared at the yeti strings on her violin. They still glowed with a faint blue light. "Whoa!"

As Yi started down the path that would take her away from the Buddha, Jin came up behind her. "Yi!" he said sternly. Yi turned around. *Now what?* He handed her one of the flowers and grinned. "We are so going to the Himalayas." Yi smiled and carefully tucked the flower into her violin case.

They climbed down the Buddha statue. Yi looked back up at it before they left. The setting sun cast an orange halo around the Buddha's head, and a heaviness inside her, one that had been there a long time, lifted.

Her dad had heard her. She knew that he loved her. Nothing would ever be the same, but she would be okay.

They began their journey to Mount Everest. Though they knew it was still a long way, they were all in a good mood. The sky grew dark and stars glittered overhead as they traveled across a grassy meadow.

Yi lagged behind to gaze at the stars. She focused on the brightest star she could see. It pulsed with light, and Yi knew her father would always be there, watching over her.

The temperature dropped as they got closer to the mountains. Eventually, they came to a grove of wisteria trees. A few months before, their drooping branches would have been covered with fragrant purple blossoms. But there was a light cover of snow on the ground, and the branches were bare.

Yi was disappointed. She loved wisteria. Then she looked at her violin case, and grinned.

She sat on a branch and began to pluck the strings.

"Why are we stopping?" Jin asked, but Everest understood. He started to hum softly. Purple flowers popped up all over the branches as Yi strummed her violin and the yeti hummed along.

"Hey!" Jin cried, as one of the branches picked him up. Another branch scooped up Peng. The branches carried Jin and Peng around the tree. Fireflies joined them, encircling the tree with a warm glow.

The duet faded, and Yi climbed down from the

tree and tucked her head into Everest's warm fur. Peng did the same.

"Come on," Jin urged them. "If we keep going, we'll get to the Himalayas by morning. Those guys are not going to stop until they get—"

Everest yanked Jin over to the group and into the warmth of his fur.

"Is that better?" Yi asked.

"Maybe," Jin admitted. "We still have to keep going, though."

"I know," Yi said.

"Will it be the same?" Peng asked. "You know, when Everest goes home? With us, I mean. Like, will you guys still want to hang out?"

"Of course we will, Peng," Yi said.

Jin gazed up at the sky. "You know, I'll sure miss seeing these stars."

"Yeah, but even though we can't see them, we'll still know they're there," Peng said. "So that's kinda cool, isn't it?"

Yi smiled. "Yes Peng, that's very cool."

The stars watched over them as they had a short rest. Then they walked all night, and finally they reached the foothills of the Himalayas. A light snow fell as they walked up a ridge.

"It's not funny," Jin was saying. "Loch Ness monster? Chupacabra? What if they exist? Oh my gosh, my whole life has been a lie."

They reached the top of the ridge, and the snow-covered Himalayas came into view. Everest hooted with delight, and Peng fist-pumped the air.

A wooden suspension bridge stretched out in front of them, connecting the ridge to the mountain range. The bridge crossed a dangerous, deep chasm.

"Everest, look! Just across that bridge is home!" Yi told him.

"What are we waiting for?" Peng asked. "Let's go! Let's go!"

They headed into a tunnel that led down to the bridge. Everest emerged first, eagerly galloping across the bridge, excited to be almost home.

"Everest, wait up!" Yi called out.

Vroooooooooom! A loud, whirring sound filled the air as two Burnish Industries helicopters cut across the sky. They landed on the far side of the bridge, blocking the way.

"Go back!" Yi yelled.

Guards spilled out of the helicopters and came

toward them, armed with stun guns. They turned to go back to the tunnel, but a fleet of SUVs and an armored transport vehicle poured out, blocking their way. Yi, Peng, and Jin stared at one another in terror. Everest looked worried.

They were trapped!

Chapter Thirteen
No Escape

Everest opened his arms, protecting his friends. But Yi pushed him toward the mountains.

"Everest, run! Go to your mountain before it's too late! You can get past those guys!" she yelled.

Behind them, Mr. Burnish stood next to a yeti-size cage on the back of a truck.

"Captain, hurry!" he barked. "Get my yeti! Get him now!"

Everest turned to Mr. Burnish and growled. Then he ran back toward the tunnel. When he got close, he climbed up to the top of the bridge and hummed.

Storm clouds swarmed in a circle above him. The wind howled, and the night sky flickered with a blue light. Lightning struck the bridge, and the wind pushed the guards backward.

"Mr. Burnish, we're missing our chance!" Dr. Zara warned.

"Load the tranquilizer guns!" the security captain ordered.

"Locked and loaded," one of the guards reported.

Mr. Burnish stared up at the yeti, amazed by his powers. He held up his hand.

"Wait, hold your fire!" he ordered, and the puzzled guards obeyed.

The lightning flashed, sparking Mr. Burnish's memory. He remembered a day forty-five years ago when he was a young explorer, full of curiosity and wonder. Climbing Mount Everest, he had stumbled upon a giant footprint in the snow. He reached down to touch it, and when he looked up, a giant yeti stood in front of him.

Terrified, he had swiped his ice axe at the creature. The beast leaped back, revealing three smaller yetis cowering behind it.

At that moment, Mr. Burnish realized how

terrified those creatures were of him. He wanted to reassure them, reach out to them somehow. But then there was a hum and a flash of blue light. Snow whipped up all around him, and when it cleared, the yetis were gone. Even the footprint had disappeared.

Kablam! Lightning struck nearby, rousing Mr. Burnish from his memory. He gazed up at Everest, and the three kids he was protecting.

"Mr. Burnish," Dr. Zara prodded, but he didn't respond. Desperate, she turned to the guards.

"Take the shot!" she demanded.

Mr. Burnish looked up at Everest, then back toward the kids. "He's defending them," Mr. Burnish said. He turned to Dr. Zara. "Doctor, I was wrong, you were right. The yeti must be protected, and the best way to protect the yeti is to let him go."

He threw down his ice axe. "We must let him go," he repeated, his voice rising. He turned to his captain. "Captain, order your men to stow their weapons! Do it now!"

Unsure, the security captain looked to Dr. Zara. The wind whipped her hair around her face. She nodded to him.

Zip! He shot Mr. Burnish with a dart from the

tranquilizer gun. The man's eyes closed. Dr. Zara rushed to him, removed the dart, and shoved it into her pocket.

"Quick! Mr. Burnish needs help!" she cried.

Guards swept in and carried Mr. Burnish to the SUV. Now Dr. Zara was in control.

"Captain!" she commanded.

The captain shot another dart at Everest. He stopped humming. The magical storm stopped.

"Fire at will!" the captain shouted.

"Fire!" the guards repeated.

They bombarded Everest with tranquilizer darts.

"No!" Yi yelled.

The darts hit the yeti from all sides. He struggled to keep his eyes open, but the tranquilizers were too much for him. Losing his balance, he tumbled off the top of the bridge and landed hard on the deck.

Yi, Jin, and Peng ran to Everest's limp body, but the guards stopped them, grabbing them by the arms. They watched helplessly as more guards put Everest in chains and dragged him to the iron cage.

"No!" Yi yelled, struggling to get away from the guard holding her.

"Everest!" cried Peng, kicked his guard in the shin.

"No, no, Everest!" Jin cried, but he couldn't break away either.

Dr. Zara grabbed a stun gun from the captain.

"I'll make sure the yeti's out," she said in her real voice. "He is never going to escape again!"

She started to press the stun gun against Everest's body. "STOP!" Yi shouted.

She broke free from the guards holding her and lunged at Dr. Zara. She grabbed Dr. Zara's arms, trying to wrestle the stun gun away. The woman pushed Yi hard, sending her teetering toward the edge of the bridge. Jin and Peng watched in horror as Yi fell over the railing and disappeared into the mist! Her backpack and violin remained behind on the deck of the bridge.

Chapter Fourteen
Yi's Song

"Noooooooooo! No! No!" Jin wailed.

"Yi!" Peng had tears in his eyes.

The guards pushed them both into the back seat of one of the SUVs, next to an unconscious Mr. Burnish. Dr. Zara turned to the security captain. "Well, that's one down." She climbed into the driver's seat and gunned the engine.

"No, go back! Stop the car!" Jin shouted. He pounded on the car window.

But the vehicle moved into the dark tunnel, back toward the city.

Jin stared out the window, frozen in shock. Everest was captured. Had he just lost Yi forever? The convoy drove away.

Yi's violin case was open on the deck of the bridge. Her postcards and photo of her dad fluttered away in the wind. All seemed lost when suddenly a voice could be heard, struggling. It was Yi. She'd managed to grab onto one of the bridge supports when she fell. She reached for a beam with one hand, but her other hand started to slip.

Yi's heart sank as postcards floated down all around her and disappeared into the chasm below. They had come all this way, and things were worse for Everest than ever before. And there was nothing more she could do.

It's hopeless, she thought.

And then the white flower she had tucked into her violin case fluttered down from the sky and landed on her arm. It was a small thing, but it gave her hope.

Using every bit of strength she had, she pulled herself up to the beam above her. Then she pulled herself up to the next, and the next, until she was back on the deck. She picked up her violin and locked her eyes on the path moving through the foothills, until she saw the convoy of Burnish Industries vehicles— and the cage holding Everest. They were on a road in the hills, bordered by a mountain on one side and a steep cliff on the other.

She lifted the violin to her chin and began to play. The strings of yeti hair began to glow and spark. The sky flashed with blue light, just as it had when Everest hummed.

This was no sweet song of love. She played with fierce intensity. As the notes became faster and louder, lightning flashed. The blue glow in the sky pulsated like the Northern Lights.

Tweeeeeeeeeeeeeeeeeeeee! Yi hit a high, piercing note, and sustained it. In response, a single blue ribbon of light whipped around her, as if it was absorbing the energy from her music. Then the light raced through the valley, aiming at one target—Everest!

The blue light ribbon surrounded Everest's cage. His body glowed, and it became so bright that everyone in the convoy had to shield their eyes. The yeti's eyes flashed open.

Rooooooooar! He burst through the iron bars of the cage. Huge stalagmites burst from the road in front of the vehicles, rising up like giant icicles. The drivers had to swerve and brake to avoid hitting them.

Dr. Zara's SUV screeched to a halt as a stalagmite erupted in front of it.

"It's Everest!" Peng cheered.

Dr. Zara emerged from the vehicle. "No, this can't be happening!"

Everest stood tall, glowing brighter than ever before. More stalagmites burst from the ground. The guards began to run away, and Dr. Zara sprinted toward the transport vehicle.

Jin gently shook Mr. Burnish.

"Sir, wake up!" he urged. But the man was out cold.

Duchess climbed out of Mr. Burnish's pocket and hopped onto his chest. Her tiny, twitching nose tickled his face. Mr. Burnish's eyes fluttered open, and the rodent squeaked.

Jin and Peng helped pull Mr. Burnish out of the SUV just as Yi slid down a giant stalagmite to join them. Jin couldn't believe his eyes.

"Yi! You're okay!"

Yi smiled and turned toward Everest. They exchanged a knowing look. Yi felt strong and proud.

With Everest's powers and her violin, they were unstoppable!

Then the roar of an engine interrupted them. The transport vehicle barreled toward them, with Dr. Zara behind the wheel and the security captain beside her. With its armored body and monster wheels, it pushed past the vehicles and mowed down the stalagmite. With wild eyes and hair whipping around her face, Dr. Zara stomped on the gas, aiming for Everest.

"I thought we had to keep the yeti alive," the captain said.

"DEAD will have to do," Dr. Zara replied.

"No!" Yi yelled, and she jumped aside as the vehicle barreled toward them.

Dr. Zara slammed into Everest, pushing the yeti into the mountain wall.

"Yes!" she exclaimed.

Cr-a-a-a-a-ck!

A crack erupted in the ice covering the mountain's face. It raced up toward an overhang of snow. The mountain rumbled, and an avalanche of snow swept down the mountain, carrying the transport vehicle—and the yeti—over the cliff.

"Noooooooooo!" Dr. Zara wailed, and then the

snow settled, and an eerie silence fell over the valley.

Yi, Jin, Peng, and Mr. Burnish rushed to the edge of the cliff. Nobody could tell for certain what exactly had happened.

"Everest?" Peng called out.

Chapter Fifteen
Flight

Behind them, they heard a familiar coo. They turned to see Everest emerge from a snowbank and walk toward them. He had not gone over the cliff after all.

"Everest?" Yi hugged him, and Peng joined in. Even Duchess gave a happy squeak.

Mr. Burnish approached the yeti. "Everest? You are by far the most extraordinary creature I have ever seen. That is exactly why the world must never know you exist." Everest looked at him curiously. "They would not understand. I didn't," he explained.

Mr. Burnish turned to Yi. "Can I please help you to

get back to the city? It would be my great pleasure."

"Thank you, but I promised to take Everest home, and he's not home yet," she replied.

Mr. Burnish shook his head. "You're not going to take Everest all the way to Everest? That is impossible."

"Sir, with all due respect, when Yi sets her mind on something, nothing is impossible," Jin informed him.

Mr. Burnish nodded. "I understand," he said. "But there is something I have to insist that I give you."

He walked up to his security guards and got three of them to give up their winter gear. Soon Yi, Jin, and Peng were decked out in parkas, gloves, and hats.

"Thank you! See you later!" they called to him, as they headed back to the tunnel.

"Don't worry. I'll be waiting right here," Mr. Burnish promised.

Peng stopped and looked up at the tallest mountain in the distance. "It sure is a long way up there."

"Everest?" Jin asked.

Everest shut his eyes and started to hum. The clouds overhead began to join together, forming shapes resembling giant koi fish.

"Cool!" Peng said.

The clouds swooped down, ready to carry them to the mountaintop at Everest's command. Yi looked at Jin. Would he take the leap this time?

Jin opened his arms wide. "Bring it!" He finally trusted the yeti's powers.

The clouds enveloped them, and then broke up again into koi fish shapes. Jin rode one cloud, and so did Peng. Everest and Yi rode together. They whooped and cheered and the clouds leaped in and out of the churning mountain mist, like koi swimming upstream.

Soon the clouds parted, revealing the peak of Mount Everest.

"Everest, it's your mountain," Yi said, and the yeti cooed with gratitude.

It got colder and colder as they neared the top of Mount Everest, and the three humans were happy for the winter gear that Mr. Burnish had provided them. High winds whipped snow around the peak as the clouds deposited them on a flat spot.

"What do we do now?" Peng wondered.

"I don't know," Yi answered honestly.

Everest knew what to do. He hummed. His body pulsed with a faint blue light.

Then he paused. A soft hum responded. Suddenly, there was humming all around them!

Blue lights became visible through the swirling snow. They pulsed brighter and brighter as they grew closer. Yi, Jen, and Peng watched in awe as a group of yetis emerged through the snow. Each one of them was five times as big as Everest.

"Wow. They would be SO good at basketball!" Peng exclaimed.

Two of the yetis came closer to the group. Yi smiled.

"His parents," she said.

Everest beamed at them, but then he turned back to Yi. She shyly stepped forward.

"You're finally home, Everest," Yi said, forming a triangle with her hands. "Home."

Everest pulled her hands to his heart and cooed.

Yi suddenly felt sad. "I can't believe the journey's over."

Everest shook his head. He let go of Yi's hands, and she realized he had placed something in them. It was the photo of her father that she kept in her violin case. But it wasn't *just* a photo of her dad. The photo had been slid into a pocket in the violin case and only showed Yi and her dad. But now the other half of the photo was revealed. It was the whole family—Yi, her dad, her mom, and NaiNai. . . . Her eyes welled up. She missed them all so much! Yi's heart pounded as she focused on Mom and NaiNai. She longed to see them. She longed to go home.

"You're right. It's not over," she said. She pressed her forehead against his. "Thank you, Everest."

They hugged, and Peng ran up to join them.

"I'll never forget you, Everest!" he promised.

Jin approached with his hand held out. Everest pulled Jin in for a hug. The group hug lasted a long time, until they finally pulled away from one another.

With a happy cry, Everest ran toward his family. Two giant yeti paws reached down and scooped him up. His parents engulfed him in a warm embrace. The two huge yetis looked down at Yi and gave her a grateful nod, and Yi nodded back.

Then all of the yetis began to hum. The wind and snow whipped up around them. Yi focused on Everest's face for as long as she could, until the yetis disappeared in a flurry of snow, leaving no trace behind.

"Now it's our turn to go home," Yi said.

I came all this way to help Everest find his family, she thought. *But Everest, and Jin, and Peng . . . they've helped me find my way back to mine.*

Chapter Sixteen
Home

Two days later, Yi, Jin, and Peng arrived back at their apartment building, traveling in style in a Burnish Industries SUV.

Yi raced inside first—then stopped to look at Jin and Peng. They had all been through so much together. She remembered Peng's questions. *Will everything be the same when we get back? Will we still hang out?*

Jin smiled at her, and she knew the answer. Their Everest adventure had brought them all closer together. It was a bond they'd never forget.

With a nod to Jin, she bolted up the stairs and into her apartment. Her mother looked up from her computer and stood to greet Yi.

"Oh, Yi, you're back. How was the trip?"

Yi wrapped her arms around her mother, whose eyes widened in surprise. It had been a long time since her daughter had hugged her. Then NaiNai entered the room.

"Yi?" she asked, just as surprised.

"I missed you both so much," Yi said.

"It's good to have you back, Granddaughter," NaiNai said.

Yi knew what her grandmother meant. She *was* back, heart and soul, and it was a good feeling.

"This calls for a celebration," NaiNai said. "I will make some pork buns."

"Yes!" Yi agreed. "And we need to invite Jin and Peng, too."

Her mom raised her eyebrows again. "Of course!"

A few hours later, NaiNai was arranging steamed pork buns on a platter, and Yi's mom was preparing the dipping sauce. The doorbell rang, and Yi ran to let in Jin and Peng, who was carrying a large box.

"Look what I found on your doorstep," Peng said.

"It's addressed to all of us! What do you think it is?"

"Shhhh!" Yi warned. She looked over her shoulder to make sure her mom and NaiNai hadn't heard. Then she ushered the boys into the living room. They huddled around the box, and Yi carefully lifted the lid.

Inside was a bunch of climbing gear—jackets, ropes, harnesses, and three ice axes. On top was a note: *For your next adventure. Burnish.*

Their mouths dropped open.

Yi's mom called to them from the kitchen. "Hey kids, how was Beijing?"

Yi quickly put the lid on the box and shoved it under the sofa.

"It was, uh . . . life-changing," Jin answered. Yi smiled at him, and Peng burst into giggles.

"Wow, that's great. Are you all ready for dinner?" Yi's mom asked.

"Yes please!" Peng said.

They all helped bring plates and platters to a small table in the living room.

"Everybody dig in!" NaiNai said.

Jin and Peng chowed down on the pork buns.

"Wow, I totally see what you mean about these

pork buns, Peng," Jin said. "They are incredible."

"There's no one in the whole world who likes these pork buns more than me," Peng said.

"Well, maybe one," Yi said.

She turned to look at the violin propped up on a shelf in the corner. The white yeti hairs glistened.

"Who? Who else likes my buns?" NaiNai wanted to know, and everyone laughed.

"No laughing. I'm serious!" NaiNai insisted.

But that only made them laugh even more, and their laughter floated out of the window, up above the rooftops of the city, and into the night sky, where one star shone the brightest of all.

THE END